BENEATH THE CICADAS' SONG

Alli —
Thank ya so
much for yar
support.

BENEATH THE CICADAS' SONG

Lindsey Doyle

NEW DEGREE PRESS

BENEATH THE CICADAS' SONG

ISBN

978-1-63676-864-9   *Paperback*
978-1-63730-178-4   *Kindle Ebook*
978-1-63730-308-5   *Digital Ebook*

For Raquel and my parents, Mary L. and John C. Doyle

SENSITIVE CONTENT WARNING:

Please note that this book contains suggestive and graphic content related to violence, self-harm, substance abuse, sex, domestic violence, and eating disorders.

This book is not intended for young readers.

Based on psychological research and best practices for depicting self-harm in literature, reader discretion is advised.

CONTENTS

———

AUTHOR'S NOTE

—

I was on plastic bag duty, too short at the time to reach the food counter to serve people coming for their one hot meal that week. At eight years old, I crouched behind the counter staring at people's feet, pulling used plastic grocery bags from a bigger trash bag, and balling them up as small as I could. Once they had their food, I was told to walk around the lunchroom and give one to each person.

My parents had taken my brother and me to one of many homeless shelters in Los Angeles with our church. We would often take service trips from our suburban home to South Central Los Angeles. My parents were gradually and lovingly instilling in us the basic yet transformative idea that even if we experience challenges in our lives, we came from privilege that could be used in the service of others.

Children of highly accomplished and socially grounded parents, my brother and I had won that irreverently unfair lottery of birth, so we served because we could.

Later, I learned the plastic bags were for people to use to go to the bathroom so they wouldn't defecate in the streets.

Plastic bags? Was that the best they could offer?

I longed for a different answer.

I was witnessing marginalization and a well-meaning support system that was utterly overwhelmed. Together, they highlighted the indignity of living on the margins of society.

By 2030, 40 percent of people living in cities worldwide will reside in slums.[1] The agenda of the urban, marginalized poor is one that continues to be pushed to the side, in part because their stories remain unheard, because there are powerful financial and institutional interests that want it to stay that way, and because when the opportunity arises for a community to act together against that power, the struggle to live and keep one's family alive takes precedent over the collective. With climate change, the long-lasting impacts of COVID-19, and the myopic return of nationalism, the pressures on those experiencing poverty only continue to mount.

Progressing through my early career as a policymaker and advocate, it became clear that the world isn't fair—an obvious realization that lodged itself deep in my core. I saw many examples of brutality that sent the message that marginalization wins. I watched as governments, nonprofits, and social enterprises all struggled, with mixed success, to make a difference. Existing policies and approaches to deal with such immense global issues always seemed to fall short. The complex political dynamics that generated inequality, racism, suffering, and oppression were no match for their will.

My early response to this stark mismatch was a kind of quiet guilt and self-sacrifice for any work that seemed to bend that arc of justice. It was somehow all my responsibility because I was paying attention. Overworking was rewarded and the need was vast, so I just never stopped.

---

1   Abrahm Lustgarten, "The Great Climate Migration Has Begun," *The New York Times Magazine*, July 23, 2020.

From 2013 to 2014, I had the opportunity to work in two low-income communities in San José, Costa Rica (Triángulo de Solidaridad and Los Cuadros), where thousands of Nicaraguan families had settled, initially because of Hurricane Mitch in 1998 and the lack of economic opportunity in Nicaragua left in its wake.

I started working with the residents of the community in an attempt to understand their lives and to connect with them. I didn't set out to write a book, yet over the course of the six hundred hours I spent working there, I accompanied and interviewed more than fifty people who had experienced the sharper edges of what life can throw. These moments of connection in their own language happened in the walkways of their communities, on the bus, in their homes, and in community centers supported by the Boy With A Ball Foundation.

The process of accompanying the people living these realities awakened me to the power of personal narrative, particularly in the context of building resilience. When they told their stories, it was as if they no longer had to withstand the weight of them all by themselves. In listening to other people, we have a chance of understanding what they have endured and acknowledging that no matter one's life experiences, we are inextricably linked. While the systems that allow marginalization to take root are the products of many purposeful, and sometimes mindless, decisions over time, we have the individual power to stand in solidarity with them. Empathy dissolves fear. Community removes otherness.

Inspired by their stories, I also documented events, personalities, and settings using participant observation, photography, and voice and video recording when given consent. I researched secondary sources from government documents, diagnostics collected by nongovernmental organizations (NGOs), academic reports, and newspaper articles to fill in the gaps. I visited three other low-income communities in Alajuelita, San José, Roble-alto, Heredia, and Playa Potrero, Guanacaste. The organizations that hosted me were the Nicaraguan Women's Network (Red de Mujeres Nicaragüenses), Center for Mediation and Conciliation (Centro de Mediación y Conciliación, CEMEDCO), and Opening Minds (Abriendo Mentes).

In writing this book, I also drew on my knowledge and experience from ten years of work on global development and justice issues, peace and conflict research, and the political and social inner workings of societies across Central and South America. This book is fiction, though it is based on true events from these communities that I either witnessed or were told to me by residents. Any character's likeness to real people is purely coincidental.

On one of my last days in Triángulo, Raquel, a tireless young leader who lived and volunteered there, walked me from the community center through the narrow passageways out into the adjacent neighborhood where I would catch the bus home. She was accompanying me, taking care to make sure I made it safely.

I boarded the bus, sank coins into the meter, and found a seat on the left by the window. As the bus pulled away, I watched Raquel descend back down the street toward the tin roofs that melted off the hillside into piles of trash. They called it a *precario*. Heat welled up in my chest and came out my eyes. I knew I would never really know her struggle. I was a mere visitor, a guest in her home, invited simply to listen, acknowledge, and be.

Like the eight-year-old huddled beneath the food counter fumbling with plastic bags, I felt a deep sense of insufficiency. Immense global challenges and tensions made it personal: I would never be enough. Not now, not ever. It was a familiar sadness and one that fed the guilt that somehow justified how little I served my own mental and emotional needs for someone expecting to stay in the social justice ring past the tenth round. It was a dangerous, naive approach, and one that, I have come to learn, is very common among people drawn to service. Thankfully, I am not unique.

Like so many of us who imagine a more equitable and just future for our neighborhoods, cities, and world, we often forget the power to change is always within us. We can take the time to understand and feel an ounce of what another person has experienced. It is the ordinary act of presence.

In January 2020, I received a Facebook message with a picture of a front yard and a patio with potted flowers. Below the photo, it read:

> "You have been a great friend to me. I want to thank you for all your support. I remember our conversations, and I want to tell you that one of my dreams has come true, thanks to people like you believing in me. My family had the opportunity to buy a house, and now we don't live in a slum anymore. I so appreciate your friendship and wanted to share my happiness with you. We've had a hard time as a family, and I know I haven't responded to your many messages. But I value how you always cheered me up. Thank you for this. You are a piece of this success."[2]

---

2   Translated Facebook direct message to author, January 29, 2020.

It was from Raquel. It had been years; a distant experience, suddenly revived by a sweet, simple reminder of friendship. She had bought a house for her family—a game changer in social mobility—making the long, difficult journey out of the slum.

Ultimately, guilt will not dismantle the global power structures that keep people down. The impulse to control will not make a wrong, or ten thousand of them, right. Self-denigration does not make us more capable of fighting for and living out our values and seeing the ever-present rewards we receive for overworking ourselves as somehow indicative of our personal worth.

These are blockages bolstered by fear that rob us of the opportunity to serve—and live—to our fullest.

Instead, the portal to staying power, vocation, and lightness is interrogating our own reasons for wanting to be of service. We become capable of doing the slow, steady work of accompanying people who are living through hardship by instead acknowledging our own value and worth. By daring to empathize with people who live very different lives, we discover that we, too, are enough.

We can develop a practice of noticing and fully honoring our own needs and wants for the intrinsic benefits that brings, and we can make our entire lifetimes of work on matters of life, death, and struggle sustainable and fulfilling.

If we are to build inclusive, just societies, avert the worst of what climate change has in store for us, and continue to make monumental strides in poverty alleviation, it is about having compassion for and quieting the part of us that makes it all about us. Through this process, we release ourselves from the hubris of being the solution. We return to the humble position of the contributor.

Thank you for taking an interest in this story, for extending a hand by spending time learning about these communities now etched in my memory and hopefully yours soon, too, as they become the driving force behind our every effort to help build the future that they imagine.

PART I

ANTS' WORK

CHAPTER 1

GABRIELA

Gabriela glued her nose to the crooked wooden plank. None of the nail heads were flush. Mamá had hammered a piece of plywood to the opening at the top of the staircase. She said it was so no one fell to the first floor.

A trail of black leaf-cutter ants had adopted the plank as their highway. From the free and expansive treetop, the ants carried leaf cutouts six times their size down the inclined trunk. They marched around the sewer cover where the gray wash water flowed between Gabriela's house and the neighbor's. From there, they disappeared into a hole in the ground.

What a marvelous feat.

Mamá told her how their neighbor, Ricardo, built the second floor of their house after she and her younger sister were born. The fourth room was added just a year ago, around Gabriela's seventh birthday.

When Fernando came to stay, Mamá shifted the rooms around and built more walls out of plywood and plastic sheets, just like the faded blocks she used to play with. He was just a little thing then. *Mamá said he didn't have a mother, so we'd be his family instead.*

Mamá—Jimena, as everyone else called her—took care of a lot of kids who weren't hers. She always made sure everyone had their own space by spreading her elbows out in each room to see if they touched the walls. The room for Fernando didn't pass, so she moved the satellite dish and added another level. Nowhere to build but up, Mamá would say.

The television signal had never been the same.

Together, the ants marched in a perfect line up the tree. If disturbed, they didn't recover their path. Instead, they walked in circles around each other, forming patterns that resembled the hurricanes on TV the weathermen talked about. Unsure of where to go, they followed along, stuck like that for hours. It was best just to watch, leaving them to march in peace.

Through the small square window in the metal wall, the entire shantytown splayed out below like a crooked checkerboard. A sea of Claro and SkyTV satellite dishes perched atop rusted metal and haphazard plywood. Every year, the roofs turned a little more orange and a little less gray.

In the distance, the hotel peaked above the tin with glass windows that were always vibrant and clean. It peered down as if it had something to say. It was beautiful. Mamá called it hermetic. *Whatever that meant.*

The city train passed by every half hour on weekdays packed with people all going somewhere. The tracks separated the *precario* from the fancy people in Monte Verde.

Gabriela squinted to read the wooden sign above the next shack: "*Soda de Layla: Nacatamales, Soup: Chicken and beef, pork with yucca.*"

She could recite all the signs by heart. "*Chocobananos: 200 colones.*" "*Don't dump trash.*" "*Don't drink and drive.*" "*Water droplets crack the stone not by force, but by constancy.*" She liked the rhythm of the last one but didn't know what it meant.

From her mind's eye, she traced every long, winding corridor that had a knickknack store filled with plantains, deodorant, cleaning supplies, lollipops, milk, soda, and eggs. Gabriela's favorite was the wall of candy.

Guys with sagging jeans walked around selling fried empanadas. One neighbor sold freshly caught fish from a bucket. He was tall and gaunt and never wore a shirt.

The highway on the left buzzed. A trash fire burned at the bottom of the hill. It would go for hours atop tires and used gas cans. The smell of rotting trash was better than burning plastic, but both made her nauseous. Workers collected trash on the fire road twice a week. Some people in their part of the *precario* didn't carry theirs over there; they'd dump it over the edge of the hill, letting it tumble down to the highway's edge.

A Palanco tree grew against all odds in the middle of the pile. There must be super ants there, too.

Below, her mother swept the dirt pathways in front of their shack. She traced her mother's every move. Across the way, a pit bull lived in a wooden box. Every day, he yanked his chain and barked. Fearing one day the chain would give way, Gabriela dodged the beast every time they passed. Mamá didn't seem to mind him.

Gabriela leaned backward, her knees folding under her the way only a child's could. Her smooth belly brushed the rough underside of the plank as she slid beneath it. She cascaded down the steep stairs, landing with both feet and shaking the whole house.

In the living room, a topographical map of Costa Rica with all its groves and gullies hung above her on the wall. She couldn't quite reach it. *Maybe that was on purpose.* The map was her favorite thing in the room. A crooked picture of the *Last Supper* adorned the other.

Gabriela turned a tight corner and scampered down the metal ladder onto the concrete floor and out the front door. She mustered one of the only sounds she could make.

"Aaaaaaaa!"

Gabriela flailed about, throwing her body from side to side. Mamá turned her head to look and kept sweeping.

Was she invisible?

Gabriela ran up, bumping her mother's leg with her little body, whining and touching her hand to her open mouth. She didn't have a voice like all the other kids. Mamá said it was her special gift, but sometimes it was hard to feel that way.

"You're fine, *mija*! You just ate," Mamá said.

Gabriela grunted back. She *had* just eaten, but it was always worth a try. Mamá didn't let her get away with much.

Mamá pounded her rubbery Styrofoam Croc into the ground, jolting Gabriela from her moment of self-pity. A cockroach wiggled beneath her mother's shoe. In an unusual moment of focus, Gabriela knelt down, peering at her mother's feet pattering around. She watched as ants flocked to the scene and started to pick up the mess.

Gabriela loved that she could see, even if she couldn't talk. There were so many things to look at and wonder about. Her mind drifted to yesterday at the center. She was learning her kind of words.

"Car," her sign language teacher said, scooting a chair up in front of Gabriela. She had long, jet-black hair that didn't move much when the wind came.

Gabriela extended her arms with her hands in fists, as if holding a steering wheel, and swayed back and forth.

"Good! Next one: 'tired.'"

Gabriela took a deep breath, arching her back as her lungs filled with humid air. Wiping her hands down her protruding stomach, she let it all out and slumped in her chair, smiling.

"So good! How about 'bubbles?'" Her teacher had an upbeat tempo about her, relentlessly positive.

Not quite able to coordinate her index fingers and thumbs, Gabriela grasped at the air, batting and folding her hands erratically, making the sign for bubbles.

"Ooopa!"

Gabriela loved her teacher and wished she could play that game forever. *How many words are there in the whole wide world? Two hundred? Maybe five hundred?* Gabriela was convinced she would learn them all.

Mamá tossed the chain through the hole in the plywood door, startling her from the daydream. Gabriela looked down at her feet. The cockroach remains had vanished.

Ants had no sense of sight. It was as if they smelled death instead.

CHAPTER 2

CRISTINA

At their kitchen table, Cristina pushed *gallo pinto* from one side of her plate to another. Across the room, Jacob's eyes bugged out of his head as their mother, Vivia, bounced him on her knee in a rocking chair made of stretchy lime green plastic across the room. Their little sister Belén played on the floor.

Cristina masticated the same ball of mushy rice and beans around in her mouth. The sensation of the pulp squeezing against her cheeks made her queasy. She didn't dare swallow.

Cristina peered up at her sister, Patricia, sitting kitty-corner at the table, reading. At fourteen, Patricia was two years younger than Cristina, but now in same middle school grade. *She'd be two ahead in no time if Ma would ever enroll us again.* Cristina's bare feet were cold against the packed dirt floor, but it felt good in the summer.

Their neighbor, Xianne, walked in and sat down at the same table with her back to Cristina. She left the front door ajar, illuminating all the useless, suffocating stuff piled up in their corrugated house. An entire wall of plywood shelving was lined with used clothes she never wore, plastic food containers stacked several feet high, old car parts, buckets, broken chairs, and junk upon more junk enclosed in a dark entryway made visible only by their unwanted visitor.

"How's it goin'?" Xianne said. She wore too much leopard print for her heavy body type.

"Alonso wants me to work," Ma said.

"Mhmm." Xianne pursed her lips. Cristina guessed she knew a thing or two about men.

Jacob arched his back and started to whine. Vivia held him under his armpits as he squirmed. Xianne looked on. She seemed content with herself that Jacob wasn't hers. *Just you wait, another kid will be on the way. They always are.*

"You know, I've never regretted having children," Ma said.

Jacob climbed up to the top of the rocking chair, throwing his little arms around Ma's neck like a koala bear cub.

"I'll bet you don't," Xianne said.

"Alonso gets so bored with the kids. He can't spend more than half an hour with 'em."

Xianne scrunched her upper lip toward her nose, nodding.

"Patricia! Bring me a popsicle for Jacob!" Ma aimed her command toward the makeshift kitchen.

Patricia emerged a moment later handing her mother a bright red popsicle wrapped in clear plastic. Ma paused to open it. Excited, Jacob stood up in his mother's lap, digging his little feet into her thighs. His diaper, a size too big, sagged on his thin body. Jacob grasped the popsicle with both hands and licked it up and down. Sugary red coloring painted his lips, chin, and cheeks. The musty humidity melted the popsicle until juice crept down his hand and dripped off his tiny elbow onto his mother's lap.

"What hurts me most is when Jacob tells me he's hungry." Ma turned her head away from her son as she said it, as if Jacob didn't know his own hunger. "But with this and milk, he should be fine to sleep through the night."

"Poor thing," Xianne said, like she didn't mean it.

"The other night they all went to bed without dinner."

Ma was airing their dirty laundry with a woman who didn't give two shits.

"It's been really hard." Ma showed more emotion than Cristina could bear. Cristina rolled her eyes at her mother's show of vulnerability. *No one needs to know our business, and we're doing just fine.*

Cristina ducked her head beneath the edge of the table, spitting the chewed-up food into her hand and letting it slide off her palm onto the floor. She scooted her chair in to cover the mess. Her dog Roger came by to lick it up. Cristina wiped her hand down her jeans that never quite fit right.

"Ma!" Cristina planted her elbows on the table with her hands on her jawbone. If she hit just the right tone, she knew her mother would acquiesce.

"Can we *please* go downtown?" Cristina said, tilting the question upward. She hated being in the house to hear her mother talk about how she wasn't eating.

Her mother glanced at Xianne and back again, waiting, as if that were any defense. *Ma just lets things happen. This time wouldn't be any different.*

"Sure, *mija.*"

"Let's go!" Cristina shrieked at her sister. A momentary victory, Cristina leapt up from her chair at the table, scraping her knees on its underside.

Patricia hung back, a capless pen still in her hand. She teetered it back and forth between her fingers and looked at their mother for approval.

"Go, *mija*, she can't be left alone," Ma said.

"Okay, okay, *dale*," Patricia said, shifting her weight out of her chair without moving it.

Momentary relief. She opened the door to their metal box at the end of a street that hadn't been paved in Cristina's whole life. It was a structure that seemed to be melting off the side of a cliff more and more each day.

Cristina felt like everyone was watching her, criticizing her every move. Too fat, not tall enough. Sometimes she didn't want to be in the house, or out on the street, or anywhere really. Today was okay though.

The girls traced the route they always took. From their gravel street strewn with glass shards, empty soda cans, and another twenty shacks with the same piles of trash as theirs, they turned left. In unison, they took a right at the dead end—a map of their streets imprinted deep in their bodies. They could make this walk with their eyes closed. A large, scruffy rat binged on a pile of food scraps someone could afford to throw away. They started down the tow path, through the grass, down the embankment, toward the center, and walked past the soccer field and corner store.

They found their place at the back of the line at the unmarked bus stop—the only one for the whole *precario*. A weathered man with coarse gray hair emerged from between the dilapidated Chinese restaurant and a row of houses. Holding the neck of a handle of the only vodka they sold out there, he staggered toward the bus line. His knees buckled beneath the weight of what he'd been sipping all morning. He tripped backward over the edge of the gutter and fell as if in slow motion.

Thud!

The back of his skull struck the ground with a crack. No one in line moved.

"Sipping all morning, *ya veo!*" Another man said, laughing.

Cristina and Patricia stared as he struggled to stand again, grasping at nothing. Hearing the bus hiss over the hill, Cristina turned her head.

Olga and her sister approached. "It was either two and half hours roundtrip with you *nenas* to buy the right dog food or cleaning up after that *chucho* when he barfs up the cheap stuff," Olga said, elbowing Ariel in the waist. "I guess you're 'aight." She smiled, looking a little too proud of herself.

Patricia cocked her head and swatted away June bugs the size of ping pong balls.

"Olie, you can't cut the line like that!" Cristina said, playing up the drama to a line of people who didn't seem to care.

"*Chicas!* What's goin' on?" Olga said, ignoring the theater. Olga's long, plump legs made her tower over them. She was Cristina's age, though she had gotten her growth spurt first.

"Not much, *tranqui*, just chillin'," Patricia said.

Olga was wearing a sweatshirt too big for her body.

"Why are you wearing your *tía's* clothes?" Cristina said, half-joking that Olga was dressed like her aunt.

"I'm not!" Olga shot back.

The bus kicked up dust as it passed the line of people waiting and came to an abrupt stop. A few people filed off, including their neighbor Jimena, who volunteered at the center and was more put together than the rest. Jimena walked over to the frail body still lying in the gutter.

Cristina, Patricia, Ariel, and Olga boarded the bus and found seats in the far back. Cristina lifted her arm, resting it against the windowsill. It was just enough for the slackened cuff of her hand-me-down sweater to show her scars. While the other girls chattered about everything and nothing, Cristina stared out the window.

The man was still. Jimena knelt by his side and wedged two of her fingers beneath the man's chin against his carotid artery. He lifted his calloused hand with a faint, dazed smile, as if to wave. She placed her copper-colored hand on his chest and leaned back to stand up. As she walked away, his arm flopped back down on the concrete, and his neck twitched to the side.

Not even Jimena could save him.

CHAPTER 3

ARMON

Armon faced Toltero in the alley next to the warehouse. Weeds punched their way through the rusted fence leaning over from the weight, praying to their gods. Broken bottles were strewn across the dirt. The midday sky was full of wispy clouds.

Fifteen or so gang members and prospects stood behind Toltero. The older ones were dressed in crisp white collared shirts with just the first button fastened. The younger ones stood in front. They stared Armon down as if he were the enemy. They all wanted to watch. "*Norsa*," "*Salvatrucha*," and "Game Over" were painted in black ink around the curves of Toltero's bicep. The words moved along the contours as he wiped sweat from his forehead.

"For the length of this song," Toltero said. A few of the younger ones murmured to each other. "The last guy that did this died, so think carefully. How badly do you want this?"

What a privilege. Now seventeen, Armon had waited three years to be initiated into the family. It felt like the first time he shot a gun, years ago. First a *paro*, then a *chequeo*, and now he had a chance to be real.

When others gave themselves tattoos without permission, Armon resisted. They didn't deserve them yet. Too easily spotted by the police. Useless to his brothers who needed them to steal and maneuver undetected. A few of the *paros* had gaping scars where unsanctioned tattoos once were, cut off by other members. With this initiation, Armon had a chance to become one of them.

Toward the back of the crowd, one of the guys clicked open a CD player and dropped in a disc. He looked over at Toltero for the signal.

"What's it gonna be?" Toltero said.

Armon swallowed. His heart jumped into his throat. *It was what he wanted, right?* His hand started to tremble. He put it in his pocket to make it stop. Cortisol pumped through his veins, like the moment right before jumping off a cliff into the ocean.

Armon nodded.

Four of them lunged at him. He had no time to react. He was on the ground in an instant. The faint rattle of *bachata* played behind him. Too hard to hear from where he was, covered in bodies. Fists and feet struck his head, his stomach, his groin. There was nowhere to turn beneath it all. Chains pelted his back.

His mind began separating from his body. It wandered to the past.

The time his third-grade teacher slapped him in the face. The smell of the liquid they used to pour over their heads to get rid of lice. The day the military came to seize Grandpa's farm in Guatemala. In an instant, no way to fight back. The Mayan stories he used to tell. Dad getting asylum in the States. The look on his face the day he left. Moving to the city. The way Mom drank. Opening the door and walking out. Afraid to go home. Park benches. Public bathrooms. Awake at night on the concrete floor watching the June bugs fly into the fluorescent light. The first hit of crystal. Everything to dust.

With every blow, a memory erased, pushed down, forgotten. Pain was just a thought. Soon he'd be one of them. Rising above it all. Nothing to lose. Darkness.

～

Armon's eyes were swollen shut. *How long had he been out?* A sudden calm enveloped his chest. His eyelids flickered open just a crack. He could see a faint outline of "666" and a black fist on Damion's shirtless torso. Armon's whole body ached. Things swirled in his stomach. He felt like throwing up.

"Two weeks and he'll be fine," Damion said, sitting next to him in a squeaky plastic chair. His worn-out shoes rested on the arm of the couch where Armon's head was. All Armon could remember was the first hit to his head.

"Our *techos prestados* will get you back up and running in no time."

Armon had many times availed himself of this impressive network of civilians who willingly, and other times forcibly, lent rooms in their own homes for them to hide, plan, and take refuge.

Damion and the others stood up. One grabbed a razor and plugged it. As he lay there, getting his head shaved, he let his arm fall to the side of the couch. He felt around for a book he'd stuffed under there for safe keeping. His fingertips grazed the dry edges of the paper falling apart.

Still there.

Relief swept over his body—a momentary salve. It was *By the River Piedra I Sat Down and Wept.* Paulo Coelho. No one else knew he could read. The nights he spent homeless, Armon would find magazines and newspapers in the trash and try to make out the words. With the pictures and words repeated, they all started to make sense after a while. He wouldn't dare show this skill. Stories were his secret escape.

The buzzing of the razor stopped. One of the younger ones scooped up the hair on the floor with both hands and dropped it into a metal trash can, using his shoe to spread out what he couldn't manage to pick up.

"'Aight *chavalo,* rest up!"

They turned and left him lying on the couch. Armon folded his battered hands, one atop the other, on his stomach. Peering down, long socks, baggy jeans, and a white shirt were waiting for him by his feet—the first clean clothes he'd had in a while.

CHAPTER 4

THE BET

———

Cristina wandered around the sidewalk behind Olga, Patricia, and Ariel, who were huddled together and hunched over the outdoor ATM. They had their backs to the street.

"Dad's just a wallet. He doesn't care," Olga said, punching numbers into the metal keyboard.

Growing impatient, Cristina nuzzled her way between the others and fought the midday glare to see the cerulean screen. She was the shortest of them all.

"At least you guys have a bank account!" Cristina said, poking her head between them all to see the small electronic screen. Cristina felt the girls' unease as they laughed. The screen showed an hourglass tipping over itself, making them wait. The screen blinked white and blue: 0.00 CRC.

"Damn! Nothing! That son of a bitch. Mom's gonna be pissed," Olga said.

"Sorry, that sucks," Ariel said. Cristina looked down as they backed away from the ATM.

"It always shows up when I'm not thinking about it, never when I am," Olga said.

"You wanted it too much this time. Ya can't want things." Cristina laughed as she said it.

"*Mix y Mucho?*" Olga said, changing the subject, referring to a grocery store.

"Okay, *dale.*" Cristina tried to pick up Olga's mood.

They crossed the square surrounded by light orange buildings and the giant steps to sit on. A few boys were riding their skateboards around, their wheels clacking against the ridged concrete. Vendors displayed knockoff CDs and watches on tired brown blankets. It would rain soon, just like every afternoon, so they wouldn't be selling for long.

The girls crossed the narrow street, weaving between parked cars and passing hastily tagged graffiti. The automatic doors whizzed open. Cristina always loved that; doors that opened all by themselves when she approached. Such a nice feeling. Cristina met the cool store air with a half-smile. She turned down the candy aisle as Patricia and Ariel headed to look for more practical things. *Ma needed soap.*

As she made her way around, Cristina could see Olga pacing the aisles of the grocery store quicker than everyone else. *Such a busybody.* She stopped in front of the sodas. Cristina walked up next to her.

"Here, take it and just stick it in your bag and we'll go," Olga said. Cristina tilted her eyes up at the security cameras mounted in the corners overhead. Dusty fans struggled to keep up.

"No way. We're gonna get caught."

"Just do it. It's not a big deal. We're fucking broke anyway."

"I don't want to."

"Just do it, okay?"

"Seriously, Ol'." Cristina shot Olga a look, lowering her chin and narrowing her eyes. Olga scoffed and reached for the refrigerator handle. She indicated for Cristina to take one. Cristina rolled her eyes in concession and reached for a can.

"Girls, are you gonna buy that?" A security guard teetered over to them.

Christina clutched the top of the can in the palm of her hand, her sleeve concealing most of it.

"No!" Olga was insolent. "Stupid *paco*," she said under her breath.

"Do you know her?" he asked, looking at Cristina.

"Yeah."

"Well, you can either pay for it, or I'll call the police."

Ariel and Patricia poked their heads around the rack of processed ramen and tried not to get involved.

"I'll pay for it, don't worry," Cristina said. Olga threw up her hands, brushing past the guard.

He hung back with Cristina as the other three marched past the frozen dinners and ice cream.

"If I were you, I would've let your friend get caught," the guard said.

Cristina shrugged him off. She stood in the cashier's lane, placing the few coins in her tight jeans pocket onto the counter. She didn't even want it anymore. *Olga and her big mouth.* Cristina swiped the soda off the conveyer belt. As the glass wall slid open, the breeze of the air conditioning pushed her out the door.

"Why'd you do that?" Olga said.

Cristina stared at the ground in silence as they walked out.

"Enough, okay?" Cristina said, cracking the soda open. Patricia reached over to take some. Cristina retracted, laughing, before letting her have a sip. "At least we paid for it!" Cristina thumbed her nose up in Olga's direction.

Trying to stay four in a line, they walked down the street. That was tricky on a narrow sidewalk covered in black soot and sticky things.

Cristina peered into storefronts as they went. The mannequins had enormous boobs—way too big for their bodies. Their nipples were always erect. *Why? So unnecessary.* Their thin plastic figures cocked to the side, not quite upright. Pink lacy tops draped over them in uncomfortable discretion.

As they walked down the sidewalk, Cristina peered into the narrow arcades that stretched far away from the street into the dark recesses of the downtown buildings. There was something about bus stops and arcades. They always seemed to go together. Each one had its own cacophony of clown music. Slot machines, betting rings, Big Six, roulette, pinball, miniature basketball, dice. They had it all but seemed so dark and empty inside.

Olga stopped in front of a clothing store. She slipped inside as Cristina waited on the sidewalk. She let her gaze drift and took a long drag on the mouth of the soda can. Her drift snapped into focus. *Is that Papi?* Green light streamed from behind a hunched figure.

Distracted, she handed the soda to Ariel and paced into the gambling house. She wedged herself between an empty stool and a stout man in paint-speckled jeans. The odd mix of blue, red, and green lights illuminated the few freckles on the tip of her nose.

"Papi! How dare you!"

Startled, Alonso looked back at her. His coarse hand powdered in cement dust sunk into his lap, one hand still holding the stoic, lifeless arm of the slot machine. *Was that disappointment or guilt across his face?* Cristina didn't waste time figuring it out.

"How can you want Ma to work while you sit here and gamble us away?" She kept at him. "Fifteen thousand *colones* a month and you think that's enough?"

"Crissi, *mi amor*," he said, staring back at her.

"Ma doesn't ask for anything! Jacob goes to bed hungry every night. You happy with that, huh?"

"I . . ."

"No excuses!" There was nothing he could say. The last bit of innocence drained from her freckles.

"*Sabes que,* why don't we go grab a soda? Talk it through?" Alonso's voice was tepid and unconvincing. He extended his hand.

"No. Stay and play like you always do. What's it to us?" Cristina turned and walked away. Alonso's motionless figure sat slumped behind her.

The afternoon downpour started outside without warning.

"Let's just go. I'm done," Cristina said to Patricia and Ariel, who stood dumbstruck with the half-full soda still in hand. Christina charged out of the arcade, not waiting for the others.

Ariel tried to keep up, motioning to her sister to come outside.

"What? Why?" Olga asked, as their voices began to trail behind Cristina by several paces.

"Don't ask," Ariel said, trying to obviate her sister's question. Cristina looked back. Olga and Ariel waited beneath a store awning that didn't quite extend far enough to keep them dry.

Getting soaked, Cristina dodged cars, trucks, and dilapidated bike carts, perhaps waiting for one of them to hit her.

Three stops from home, a greasy-faced man with soiled clothes boarded with two wooden planks tethered to either side of his left leg. He handed the driver a piece of chocolate wrapped in red.

The driver nodded, signaling he could ride for free.

Pity. He couldn't curl his legs up and over the electronic counter bars at the front like the beggars usually do.

As the bus lurched away from the stop, the man introduced himself, saying something about not being a charity case. He had a story about being hit by a car and medical bills. He left his crutch at the front of the bus and wobbled his way down the middle aisle of the bus with a cardboard box filled with Tapita candy. Cristina tuned him out. His story couldn't be real. *All that extra emotion probably just to earn some gambling money. What else had he gambled away? How many more would he steal from?*

"One for five hundred *colones* or three for twelve hundred."

"Do you want one?" he said to a few passengers. He couldn't bend his left leg, so he walked sideways, sitting into his left hip. He used the back of the seats for balance.

"How 'bout you?" The man looked straight at Cristina.

She avoided eye contact. The gears of the bus grunted and snorted up the curvy hill. The man nearly lost his balance in front of her. She shifted her unapologetic gaze to the world outside the window.

With three coins in hand a few stops later, he hopped to the front of the bus, squeezing his legs between the edge of the bus and the turnstile.

"*Gracias, gracias,*" he said in the bus driver's general direction.

Cristina watched him hobble on one leg to get off the bus and go down the hill to do it all over again. *Just like Papi.*

CHAPTER 5

OLGA

———

Olga and Ariel leapt off the bus and walked through the neighborhood with the paved road and up the steep dirt embankment, winding their way home under an alluring gloam. Cristina and Patricia peeled off in the other direction up to Sector 3. Olga and Ariel passed what was once a park, now a garbage dump, covered in low-lying brown weeds. The trash piles would decompose, but the shards of glass would not. They'd just be tossed around forever until their edges wore off.

They walked past the dump and into a street lined with shacks. Above them, dozens of tangled strands of extension cords were plugged together and hung down dangerously close. The electrical poles bowed beneath their weight. Not every shack had its own hookup. Jimena lived up the fire road that started just after the bridge. Other friends lived in their same row. More metal lean-tos dotted the hillside below. A few bright blue ones made of tarp punctuated the landscape of otherwise nondescript, oxidized metal.

"What're we gonna do about the dog food?" Ariel asked.

"Just tell Mom what she already knows. Pa didn't send us the money," Olga said.

"Man, I really don't wanna go to school tomorrow," Ariel said, scuffing her worn-out shoe against the ground.

"You should be grateful to be going to school, you know." Olga loved school. It was the one place where her intelligence could shine: where it wasn't squelched.

Olga noticed a bar of blue lights perched atop a police car that had wedged its way up to their shack. She stopped and extended her arm, clotheslining her sister. Olga crouched down behind the corner of a terra cotta colored house, pushing Ariel behind her and shushing.

"What? What?" Ariel asked. She looked afraid without even knowing what it was.

"The cops."

With their backs to the house, Olga looked down at her feet. Her slip-on sandals revealed long toenails with chipped blue polish. The baggy sweatshirt draped over her curled body. It could only contain her secret for so long. Her shorts were damp from the ground. Looking in the distance toward their house and falling silent, Olga watched the officers talk to her mother in her floral cotton night gown and flip-flops. She looked shell-shocked and tired.

"Pa?" Ariel said, whispering. It seemed to pain her to say the word.

Olga shook her head.

Ariel leaned her thin body over to try to see.

"Let's wait," Olga said, elbowing her sister back to her place.

Ariel let out a sigh too heavy for a thirteen-year-old.

They sat in the dark side by side. Olga felt the outside of her thigh and shoulder touch her sister's as they waited. Their bodies melded for just a moment. They were suspended in the effervescent time between speculation and knowing, before anything had to be done or fixed. It was perhaps the only time Olga ever had.

A nearly panoramic view of the valley unfolded in front of them. Nighttime was spectacular. All the city lights glowed like glitter, vibrating in the distance. Everything was prettier from far away. The lights grew fainter as Olga tilted her gaze to the foreground where their neighborhood started and finally to pitch black as her eyes peered straight downward into the small coffee farm that flanked the *precario*. Darkness brought with it a rare serenity.

The front door closed, and the two officers turned and walked toward their car. Wanting the moment to last forever, Olga delayed as the car rolled by them. She took a deep breath.

"Okay," she said, indicating for Ariel to stand up.

Olga pressed her back against the terra cotta wall to get herself to standing. With her belly, it was getting harder to do those sorts of things. She took Ariel's warm hand in hers. She didn't do that often, but it felt right tonight. In one swift movement, Olga lunged out from behind the wall, taking Ariel with her. Olga let out a big laugh, as if they hadn't been hiding, pretending to be mid-conversation.

"Are you serious?" Olga said, returning to her dramatic, mercurial way.

Ariel picked up her sister's cue.

"I'm serious!" she said, replying with the perfectly fabricated exuberance of a little sister trying to play along.

"That's crazy! How'd you even know what to do?"

"I don't know, I just did it," Ariel said.

Their chatter bounced between the walls of the housing projects and took them to where the road ended and the *precario* began. Standing in front of their shack, Olga stuck her two fingers in the perfectly round hole in the plywood door, pulling it open as the bottom caught on the weeds growing beneath.

"*¡Hola Mamá!*" Olga stepped onto the cold tile floor. "What's up?"

Her mother sat with her back to the door on their faded couch. She didn't move.

Olga opened their refrigerator, pulling out a plastic container of sweet rice *arroz con leche* not meant for today.

"Mom!" Olga tried getting her attention. Even the florals of her nightgown seemed to droop. "What happened?"

Mom's hand slumped as she pressed her forefinger and thumb into her eyes.

Standing glued to her sister, Ariel nudged a fork between the openings Olga left as she picked at the rice.

"We've got just two days to move. The police came by just now."

"Whaddya mean?" Olga asked with a mouthful of food.

"They said our house is built too close to some purification site or somethin'. They have to fix the pipes," Mom said in monotone. "I guess we're in the way. They told me it's an order from the high court." Mom relayed the facts of the conversation from underneath her hand like she wasn't processing a single one.

Ariel shrunk into the dark corner of the living room. She was probably going to cry. Her emotions were always close to the surface. There were no embraces, no words of encouragement, nothing. That's all they had—nothing.

"But to where?" Olga asked.

"I dunno. Not here, *mija*."

Olga stared at the back of her mother's head. Olga's neck muscles grew tense and her head a little dizzy at the thought of being forced out and Mom having nothing to say. Her mother's figure slumped in front of her.

Taking the food, Olga plopped down in the one wooden chair they had around the mismatched table. The thought of blurting it out right then and there ran through her mind. *If Mom doesn't want to deal with a move, she won't want to deal with my pregnancy either. Maybe now's as a good a time as ever.*

An Argentinean soap opera played on the television in the background. Two poor, inexperienced thieves were robbing a wealthy family and catching them off guard as they entered the automatic gates at the bottom of their driveway. The night before, the matron's dinner party went awry. She ordered her cooks to throw out all the food. They dumped everything in the trash: whole, untouched pieces of meats, desserts, potatoes, vegetables, and breads.

Olga wanted desperately to control the situation, her mother, everything. Growing up meant life would get easier: life on her terms. Until then, it was abdication, indecision, inaction, and nothingness.

Having just eaten tomorrow's meal, anger rose within her as she watched the scene play out.

"No way! Who does she think she is?" Olga said, yelling at the TV so she wouldn't direct it at her mother. The question floated in the air above the static as Mom sat there unfazed.

CHAPTER 6

EARTH

——

Gabriela took a few steps toward the door to her house. Her pink galoshes squeaked underfoot. The door was closed. She stopped on her tiptoes.

Mamá must be busy.

She loved the sound her feet made, like music. Speeding up and slowing down, hopping on one foot and then the other. Each foot had a different pitch. One high, one low. Gabriela liked them all. She wandered down the fire road hitting every tone she could, hardly moving in a straight line.

Up ahead, the girls she knew gathered at the community center. She liked them but wasn't sure if they liked her back. They were taller, older, and so confident. She approached the gate to the center. It was the only building made of concrete in the whole neighborhood. Ariel waved.

"*Hola chiquilla*, whatcha doin' here?" Ariel said.

Gabriela smiled wide and thrust her whole body against the fence. Ariel pushed open the gate, giving Gabriela a big hug. It was awkward with their height difference, but no less satisfying. Ariel turned to go back inside the building.

"Don't go far, okay?"

Gabriela pumped her little arms in acknowledgment, making her way to her favorite corner of the yard surrounding the center.

Curling her legs under as she sat down, Gabriela pressed her cheek against the chain-link fence. Her short brown hair and tattered dress blew back in the afternoon breeze. She was tiny, but she felt big looking out at the shacks that lined the hillside's ridge in the distance with monochromatic clouds starting to gather. If Mamá didn't want to play, she'd hide instead. Surely Mamá couldn't find her there.

Gabriela's eyes traced the ridgeline. Eaves topped with fluffy green grass dropped off the edge into an embankment joining a barren field. All was calm at this distance. A giant landscape splayed out beyond the fence; those were places she wasn't allowed to go alone. The fence kept her safe. A boys' soccer game was just beginning on the field.

As her gaze came closer to the foreground, a young girl in a green school uniform skirt and a thin teenage boy in jeans, a T-shirt, and chains around his neck walked down the hill together hand in hand. The boy clenched the crook of his elbow around the girl's neck, pulling her in to kiss her, engulfing her face in his. The girl smiled, resistant but giddy.

As she stared through the bars, another little girl just her size was sitting in an enclosed area between the gate of her house and the closed door. She sat sideways on the single stair, reading a book with her back against the threshold. It was a space only big enough for girls like them. As she squinted, the girl disappeared into her eyelids.

Gabriela jumped as a loud crash rang out behind the center.

She stood up and walked next to the fence, rippling her fingers along the patinated chain links as she moved. They ran red from the rust. She touched her fingers to her tongue. *Salty.*

A creek ran behind the center, dividing them from everyone they didn't know in Monte Verde. Their houses were colorful and pretty with sturdy metal bars on their windows and garages.

As she rounded the corner of the building, a large yellow earthmover dug its fangs into the embankment. Chunks of terra cotta dirt tumbled into the gray water. It was one big mechanical vampire.

Gabriela squeezed herself into a little ball beneath her floral dress and crouched at the top of the slope to watch. Her hem fluttered against the tufts of grass. The truck was beaten up. It might've been shiny and yellow, but now it was speckled with dents and bruises.

Maybe the earth fought back sometimes.

The truck scooped and scraped the land, picking up piles dumped off the back of another truck, letting them tip out of their cradles onto the side of the creek. As dirt fell, the water started to swirl and swish in new directions. It grew angry, rising and battering the sod on either side. It frothed the light brown color of McDonald's coffees on the billboards Mamá always wanted but would never buy. Gabriela was enraptured by the water's movement.

Soon a cement truck joined the mover. It coughed thick black smoke into the air from its spout. Its pourer seemed ready to burst. The truck's noise pierced the sky as it backed up across the bridge. The two trucks worked together in unison, one dumping dirt and the other pouring cement.

At once, it started raining, just like it did every day. Too much. Too fast. As the sky opened up, Gabriela stayed. *Mamá said they were just God's tears coming down to bless us.*

Mamá was now outside the center's fence talking to Ricardo. He had broad shoulders and a burly chest and always wore a button-down shirt, even if it was soiled at the cuffs from the day before. He must have been older than Mamá, and he was always coming around to help. *Why doesn't he live with us?* Now within earshot, Mamá might have been able to see her there.

"They don't know what they're doin'. That ain't right," Mamá said with a quiver in her voice that seemed to come out more often these days.

"Yeah, didn't know about any construction this week," Ricardo said, stepping in closer to talk to Mamá, tucking a hammer into the leather strap around his waist. He rested his fists against his hips.

The dirt pile beneath the truck was waning as the earth-mover dumped more debris into the creek. A bus rode by on the damp pavement, its windows steaming up from the heat of the people inside. The tires kicked up bits of glass.

As the truck poured more cement over the embankment into the water, it turned white. Water started spilling over into the street on Monte Verde's side, inundating the edges of the *precario* where the tin walls met the ground. Green plastic bottles and bags floated around, along for the ride. Jimena and Ricardo looked at each other and took off running. Gabriela gasped and her chest tightened. She held her breath as her little brow furrowed.

Mamá pounded on the first door she could reach just down the hill from the center.

"You need to get out! It's flooding!" Mamá wasn't patient. She didn't wait for them to open before running to the next door a few paces over.

"*Oye!* Get out! Get out! It's flooding!"

Mamá was frantic, her voice trailing as she ran farther down the path. Gabriela longed to be by her side, running to save everyone, too.

"Those bastards!" She said it like she didn't mean for anyone to hear. *But I heard.*

Some neighbors emerged from their homes looking confused. Others didn't seem to care.

One man stuck his head out. As he saw the water encroaching, panic painted across his forehead. He yelled something unintelligible back inside the shack and motioned with his hand. Gabriela clutched the rungs of the fence and stood up.

Moments later, three kids emerged, two holding kittens with tousled and soggy fur. *The poor kittens.* As the kids rushed past him with water up to their shins, the man looked back inside. He stood motionless for an instant. Gabriela closed her eyes and imagined him forgetting what he came for, feeling the urge to return to the room where he'd remember. Fixating on him, she paused him in time with her mind. He hung his head then waved his hands in the air, ushering the kids who had already gone up the fire road. He turned, not bothering to close the hatch as water, violent and determined, poured out their front door. Gabriela wanted to cry.

More and more people opened their doors and dashed out carrying already-sodden belongings. They melted into seriousness. This was something new, something they couldn't run from.

As Mamá disappeared around the corner, Gabriela bit back tears. She closed her eyes and opened her mouth, extending it to the sky. She tried catching as many water droplets in her mouth as she could. Maybe help Mamá out a bit.

PART II

SOLDIERS

CHAPTER 7

WEB

———

Armon sat back in a lopsided pleather chair with his head turned to the left. Damion poked a needle and black ink pen into Armon's lower tricep like tiny chopsticks unable to pick anything up. The smell of rubbing alcohol swirled around them. Hunched over and methodical, Damion etched the outline of a web over Armor's elbow. His wounds were healing and crusting over. Getting his first tattoo was a quiet and spiritual experience. For a moment, he felt suspended by the fruits of his own will, not yet descending into what he knew would come. He turned his new name over in his head: Gabor. War chief. Brave war chief.

The others sat splayed out across the secluded warehouse, their muscular brown bodies pulsing through their ribbed white shirts. Hair cut short. More tattoos than Armon could ever dream of earning: *sombreros*, bulldogs, EME, MM, elaborate configurations of serpents and jaguars, naked women arching their back with huge tits and skinny figures, always there when they wanted them. It was their story made permanent for anyone to see. The day's humidity rested all around them, faint and watchful. A few sat around a broken television propped up on wooden pallets as if lounging in the living room they'd never have and pretending it still worked.

"*Qué bajonazo!* Followed that *chavalo* back to his house, running them off the road. And bam! Took all his money," one guy said.

"He deserved it, yo. What a chump," another said.

"Emptied his bank account. Maaaan he was so scared!"

"Ah *huacho*, I can't wait for Christmas, ooo! It's gonna be so dope."

"Christmas is like months away! What are you talking about?"

"I know, dawg, but we only get it once a year."

This was the first year Armon would be celebrating with the whole lot of them. The only two days a year they were allowed to get high. After all the haul he carried up and down hills through the rugged contours of their land, it was about time. They'd even bring in *anillos de seguridad*—the best security guys they had—to stand watch at the door to let the others rage without a care in the world.

He had made it into a family where he would remain forever.

Across the abandoned warehouse, the hand-built door clanked open. Sunday's living room sat up straight, jostling in their uneven chairs. Toltero walked in with purpose, as always. Armon knew he was smarter than most. Damion lifted his head from the surface of Armor's skin and turned to see him.

"*Tranquilos todos*—chill out." Toltero's soft laugh lingered. They all sighed and forced different variations of a smile. They seemed unsure of whether Toltero really meant it.

Toltero had built an impermeable wall around him of at least forty security guys and oversaw all deals in six *precarios*. No one could touch him—at least no one local. Below his security, there were the *corredores*, and below them, a savvy network of local *pucheros* that sold the finished product. *Pucheros* sometimes had their own *vigilantes*, usually kids, who would warn them of police or other threats. They all worked to make sure the supply was uninterrupted.

Fatherlike and intrepid, Toltero sidled up to Armon.

"What's good, Tolte?" Armon held the tremble of his voice as he spoke. Dogs smell fear from a mile away.

"Gabo, we need you to do a job," Toltero said, not wasting any time.

"*Dale*, at your service." Armon didn't hesitate.

"The jail crew needs some things." Toltero turned his eyes sideways. Damion slinked away, pushing his feet against the cement to roll his stool backward with needles in hand.

"I'll finish you up later, *chapo*," Damion said, serious and deferential.

Armon, cradling his red and raw elbow, turned back to lock eyes with Toltero. "I can do that."

"Knew I could count on you. You have to go alone, though, so don't you go gettin' all creative on me."

Armon curled his body up out of the reclined chair holding his hand against his arm, nudging Toltero backward. "Nothin' to worry about, sir."

The two walked out of the warehouse into the daylight. Toltero motioned toward a beat-up white Chevy. In the back, he pulled out two small flip phones and a switchblade.

"Here, get these to San Antonio by tomorrow."

Armon knew it well. He had been in jail nine times. The first time was the hardest. He was twelve and he'd been caught shooting bullets in the air over a school. He remembered how fun it was to be handed a gun and how scared he was when confronted. He'd slumped in the corner of the holding cell, grown men standing around him. He was small enough to find space to sit down in a ball so he could be a little more invisible there. Everyone else wasn't so lucky. They stood most of the time, agitated, angry at each other for what their own lives had become. It got easier. Every time in was an adventure. *Who would be in there with him? What could they plan?* A rebellion, maybe even a revolution. It was the university of the streets. His energy surged as he thought about it. Most of the guards knew him now and wouldn't turn away a little child support or an extra meal.

Armon swiped the phones and knife deep into his pockets. Toltero leaned in and grabbed his hand, pressing it against his chest in one swift movement, leaving a one hundred-dollar bill against his palm. American money was always the most sought-after.

Armon took off down the alleyway dotted with weeds and empty bottles. Emerging onto the street with cars passing each way, Armon walked past the line of gray pirate taxis and a dilapidated pallet truck carrying unripe tomatoes to the brim. He approached the first woman he saw. Leaning against a wooden telephone pole pelted with rusted staples, she seemed to be waiting for a request like this.

"*Nena!* Come here," Armon said. She seemed to recognize him, but Armon had never seen her before.

"What do you want?" Feisty yet obedient.

"Do you want to make a little cash?"

"*Qué cabrón,* no way. I'm not that kinda girl." She started to turn away.

"Wait, wait, it's not that. I mean, you're beautiful, and I would . . ." Armon stopped, looking her curves up and down. The way her breasts bulged out of her tight blue top. The things he would do to her.

"You would . . . ?" She interrupted his flow.

"I mean, you'd make it another way. Look." He lured her in closer. "We need some things delivered. You got pockets?" She looked down at her own cleavage and her tight jeans that would show anything if pocketed.

"I got three. How much and where to?" she said.

Armon was aroused by her confidence and didn't know which three she meant, but she seemed to know the drill.

"San Antonio. Two burners and a blade for a hundred, minus the cost of Saran Wrap and lube if you want to do it that way," Armon said.

She raised her eyebrows at him.

"In American," Armon said with a stutter he hadn't noticed in his voice before.

Her eyes narrowed as she chewed gum around and around in her mouth and considered his proposition.

"And what do you suggest if it falls out?"

Armon stared back as she rolled her eyes in submission.

"How will I know where to find you?" she said with fleeting uncertainty.

"I'm going with you."

The two ducked into the nearby outdoor market, dodging tchotchkes and the frills at the bottom of *quinciñera* dresses never purchased. Armon spotted an unlocked wooden fence.

"Go in there and do what you need to do." Armon placed his hand on her upper back, motioning her into the outcropping next to a dumpster. He handed her the switch blade and phones and she slipped between the wooden panels. He could see her shoes move around a little underneath.

Two young men sat hunched on the concrete wall flanking the market, unmoving as Armon paced around waiting.

She emerged, walking a little funny, and nodded to Armon. He flagged down a cab.

Standing in front of the main gates of the jail, they stood side by side peering up at the cameras aimed down at them. The woman fidgeted with her clothes and couldn't quite stand straight.

"They probably don't work anyway," Armon said, pre-empting her question. Still, they kept their heads down.

A man's voice came across the loudspeaker. "Visiting hours are later. Can't take you now."

"Look, I'm just trying to visit my brother, okay?" she said, taking charge. The voice over the loudspeaker paused. Armon knew he had picked the right one.

"My boyfriend doesn't have to come, if that's what you're worried about. It's really urgent. A family matter."

Still nothing. In the static over the line, Armon sifted through his mental list of names of guards he knew, trying to match the voice to one of them.

"Jorge? Is that you?" Armon said.

"*Sí, señor.*" The man's voice turned bashful. Jorge had to be about forty—*the age Dad must be by now.*

"You *will* let her in right now."

Another pregnant pause. The unexpected image of his dad fought the need for this job to go well. It was his first, and from Toltero directly. Dad usually felt distant and had just stopped calling once he made it to Los Angeles. He had the best of intentions, but dad would know better than anyone that life could take the best of you. Armon leaned into an imaginary microphone.

"If you don't, I'll fuck up your family so hard you won't even remember you had one. You know I work just as well in there as I do out here." He pointed his finger and jabbed the air toward the voice.

The gate buzzed, longer than it needed to. The woman glanced at Armon. She looked shocked it had worked. She pushed open the gate and winked. She walked down the concrete path, dirt and dried grass on both sides, until she disappeared behind the army green door as it slammed shut.

With his half-finished tattoo and his first job done, *creatively,* Armon felt like one of them, swimming upstream against the current, fighting for the promised land and all its bounty.

CHAPTER 8

OIL AND WATER

It poured rain that evening. Olga peered into the metal pot as it sizzled over the flat cookstove under the misty light in front of their home. She teetered on a piece of driftwood atop a patch of damp ground raised a few centimeters above the stream of rainwater and sewage that carried with it candy wrappers, beer cans, and empty rubbing alcohol containers. The orange candlelight danced along the ridges of the metal walls in small, perfect ovals behind her. The flame illuminated only part of their house.

For the second day in a row, not a single family in their section had power. A few families paid late, so they shut it off. This always happened and rarely got a rise out of anyone. Olga wanted them to want more.

There wasn't any power at the center, either. For years, Olga had been helping the National Children's Trust with some of its projects in the *precario*. It had met earlier that evening by the dim light of streetlight that shown through. The most recent drama was that the trust tried holding workshops for all the teenagers, but no one showed up. The trust was best known for putting kids into child protection, definitely worse than here, so no wonder it flopped.

Her mother paced in and out through the corrugated door with ingredients. Her sandals slapped against the mud as it flew up her calves, leaving small brown streaks. Mom leaned over and grabbed the spoon from her hand.

"Oil and water never mix, *sabes?*" her mother said, lifting the wooden spoon. Bits of half-cooked rice and tomato paste dripped off the edge, falling back into the pool of Girol cooking oil and water. It gave off a sweet fragrance.

"*Sí,* I know," Olga said, withholding as much sarcasm as she could. She half expected the rest of her Mom's spiel to follow: "*Be like oil. Let everything just roll right off you.*" Instead, she just smiled at Olga and turned to go back inside. Mom never angered at anything, like she'd always lived with so much uncertainty that nothing surprised her anymore.

Oil and water never mix, just like her and that boy.

She was fine at first. Giddy almost. With every hip movement, their pelvic bones were meeting, growing more intense each time. It was stinging. Sweat beads were forming on his back. Her hand had wiped some of them away. He was panting, with every exhale it seemed to go deep, deep, deep. She had never heard such sounds before.

Then there was silence in his voice and satisfaction in his eyes. She was lying there on her back, her legs flopped to one side. She was staring down the small space between the mattress and metal wall. He was there with her for just a moment.

She used to love the solitude of that corner. On her shelf stood the Barbie doll Papi had bought her after his first day of work at the construction site years ago. Next to it, her stack of Meade spiral-bound notebooks, every page filled. The nail polish Patricia lent her. Her workbooks for algebra. A shiny poster of the Golden Gate Bridge at sunset that read, "USA is yours to discover."

That day had been different. Now, none of those things seemed to matter. The memory left her with aching uncertainty that she'd never build a career to make everything work better. No more meetings at the center to get the littles ones in school. No more school herself. She longed to be the one wearing a perfectly pressed suit, having all the answers, and telling the men in suits what to do.

The guy's friends were already talking. It wouldn't be long before everyone knew; worse would be the look on Mom's face when she realized he had snuck in through the back and they had retreated together into the corner room when no one was around. *Why did she just let it happen? Why didn't anyone tell her it would be like this?* Olga was annoyed with herself for one little moment of weakness.

She had to keep it. Going back to the way things were wasn't an option. She didn't know the first place to turn for an abortion, and that word would get out, too.

She stared into the pot, watching how the droplets of oil floated like perfectly round islands in an ocean of rice, each isolated from the next. Some islands were big, others were small. *Forget politics.* She wanted to escape to her own island and get away from this unexploded bomb.

Mom's hand reached over to drop chopped onions into the pot. Olga's eyes burned as she stood unmoving. A hole in the corrugated metal awning let a stream of rainwater fall into the river. The water was encroaching on their cooking area faster every minute.

CHAPTER 9

SMOKE

———

An assembly of chairs lined the fire road, just a few paces down from Gabriela's house. Each plastic chair had a water bottle that collected beads of condensation and dripped into small puddles waiting to be sat on. Gabriela wove between the rows to inspect each one. She placed two fingers on the curved edge of each chair, pausing to count how many. They were smooth against her fingertips. The bottles teetered as she passed.

Two long lines of people extended from a folding table where Mamá stood with her back to Gabriela. The lines snaked down the hill, almost reaching the bridge. The people at the front crouched over to write on pieces of paper. The humidity glued a swathe of Gabriela's bangs to her forehead.

Others stood around facing the rows of chairs and fanning themselves with paper plates. *Why weren't they sitting in the chairs with the water to cool off?* Nicaraguan flags were posted along several shacks. In the distance, white vehicles with logos on them were parked on the Monte Verde side and surrounded by armed guards in unmarked uniforms.

Héctor and Ricardo stood on ladders on either side of the fire road, extending their arms to hang a sign between the wooden posts that held up all the wires. *Todos unidos en un mismo clamor, en una misma oración:* "All united in the same outcry, in the same prayer." The sign sagged as they ducked their heads to see how it looked.

A small group of people in suits walked up the hill. Several cameramen followed them carrying funny-looking three-pronged things that seemed to bump into everything.

Mamá stepped away from the table to greet them, extending her hand. One of them shook it. Mamá ushered them up the fire road. Gabriela ducked among the chairs and crawled on her hands and knees to the edge of the row to get out of the way.

Mamá showed the people to their rows. They nodded and smiled at her. No one sat down. Mamá lowered her head and walked around to the front of the chairs and picked up the microphone that was on the ground.

"Hi everyone. We're starting soon. Please gather 'round. Come closer," Mamá said, dropping the microphone to her side.

The people in suits backed up and formed a strange half-circle behind the chairs and kept their hands in their pockets.

Everyone who had been in line left their places and walked up the hill to join the others surrounding the officials.

Holding the microphone to her mouth again, Mamá said, "Dear God, we ask that you bless our visitors and bless this *barrio*."

The crowd hushed.

"Take care of its people and see its good works. Spare us as you did Nineveh. May you need not ask us where we have been. May we answer your call. Show us the way as you showed Jonah. Know we are acting only in your name. Amen."

A few people in the crowed crossed themselves, touching their right hand to their forehead, stomach, and shoulders.

Gabriela did the same. Gravel stuck to her knees as she knelt at the end of a row, her elbows carefully balanced on the arm of the chair and her hands clasped. The chairs began radiating the acrid smell of chemicals in the hot sun.

"Thank you for being here with us today. I now invite Ms. Trujillo to share a few words."

The young lady walked over and took the microphone from Mamá, pulling the cord around her like she'd done this before. Gabriela envied her confidence.

"Good afternoon, and thanks for joining us. My name is Ana Maria Trujillo, vice minister for housing."

Fair faced and thin, the vice minister wore jeans and an ironed blue-striped shirt. She couldn't be much older than her brother José.

"We understand you've been hearing about this relocation for years now," she said. "We want to recover that sense of solidarity, of social inclusion, and of commitment to the neediest that has been lost."

Next to Gabriela, a man whispered, "Daughter of the owner of Cem Construction, *sabes?*" motioning to the vice minister. Another bystander let out a small laugh from the corner of his mouth.

"We need to move away from the idea that the only way to get ahead is to engage in the utterly perverse forms of corruption that plague our country. I'm really proud that we ran a clean race with no special interests."

Someone had started up their wood-burning grill off to the left. Chicory smoke rose from behind the makeshift evangelical church that looked like just another shack: the perfect mix of sweet and savory, and there wasn't even meat on it yet.

"I'm here today to share more about the plans we have to support families to relocate from here."

A man's voice from the crowd called out, "Just like you forced people from their homes with that flood of yours!"

An audible grumble emerged. The people in suits who were still standing looked at one another.

"And telling people bullshit about some water purification site?" another said.

Paying no attention to the comments, the woman continued. "We had originally set a relocation date for the end of July, but we understand it is an unreasonable deadline for families to find adequate housing solutions. So, you'll be happy to know that we've pushed the deadline to August."

The groans subsided.

"This means families should begin to move now so we don't need to work with the police to have families removed. Land that becomes unoccupied will have a flag placed on it, indicating that others shouldn't reclaim it."

"That's not enough time!" someone yelled.

"This is about undoing the knot. For the sake of the speed of this project, it's vital you all respect those postings," the vice minister said, a little more nervous.

Another official seemed to sense the same tension and stood to take the microphone. He was much older, with dark hair and a gray suit with a tie situated right up to his Adam's apple.

"Look, living here is a public health risk for you and poses lots of problems if a disaster were to hit, or, heaven forbid, an earthquake. This is in your best interests. It's a humanitarian solution."

The official raised his voice above conversations breaking out in the sea of people. "My colleagues are passing out flyers that have more information. I'll read it aloud for anyone who's illiterate: only those families included in the census completed will be provided with subsidies."

With each sentence, he was more overtaken by the crowd's protesting.

"This area has been zoned and approved for the construction of the Northern Highway overpass. This will create the largest highway in our country, connecting us to the rest of the region and the rest of the world," he said, with more excitement in his voice.

A few of the armed guards had made their way up the side of the crowd and stood near the minister.

"The land that will be developed must be vacated by August 13. Land left unoccupied by families after they vacate cannot be used as credit for other persons, sold, rented, or lent. In the case that this occurs, the family cannot be transferred and will be immediately displaced by the police."

The official held the piece of paper right in front of his face.

"The order of attention will be regimented according to the following priorities. First, the elderly, then persons with disability, then female heads of household, then everyone else," he paused, "thank you." He extended the microphone out to the side, as if expecting someone else to take it.

Mamá stood up and took the microphone. She wound the cord around the butt of her hand and elbow.

Gabriela peered through the tunnel created by the plastic armchairs. The vice minister was slipping away, flanked by the armed guards. Other young officials dispersed through the crowd, handing out flyers. People surrounded the officials in clusters, looking desperate for information.

The officials slowly made their way down the hill toward the cars. The cameras followed them, stopping every few paces to film a few shacks, piles of rubbish, and the dark, black sewage flowing from an exposed pipe.

More smoke rose from behind the church tucked away between corrugated metal walls. It rose higher and higher above all the chairs with unopened water until it dispersed into the hot midday air.

CHAPTER 10

THREE WALLS

Olga balanced a large stitched bag of kitchen utensils on her forearms. They clanked around with each step she took. Olga peered around it to see where she was walking.

Lifting from his legs, their middle-aged neighbor, Ricardo, heaved a couch onto his back until it balanced on the fulcrum of his shoulder blades. A few teenage boys walked with them like hunchbacks through the slum lane, one balancing their kitchen table on his spine, another steadying a piece of corrugated metal, and the third carrying plastic grocery bags brimming with clothes. They meandered from side to side, still trying to flirt with the girls as they went. *Did they know she was pregnant? Would they still flirt if they did?* Ariel giggled as the boys barely balanced the furniture, skipping next to them down the glass-strewn street toward the newly cleared *rancho* behind the center.

They emerged onto the main road. The buses chugging up the hill looked like ants from far away, one by one picking up lines of people to go to work cleaning houses, constructing buildings, or repairing cars. A billboard stood stoic on its rusted metal legs above them: "*La luz más barata para que alcance la plata.* Vote Otto Martínez! Cheaper electricity so you can make ends meet." *The politicians just don't get it.* Maybe she would stay angry enough at their empty promises that even being a mother wouldn't hold her down. Maybe she could make things different one day.

They crossed the street and made their way to the new part of the *precario* located down the hill from the rest, behind a fence that separated the poor from the poorer. The metal door was locked. One of the boys dropped the table and jumped the fence to fetch the key, giving off a whiff of their pubescent odor. Olga did her best to crack a smile at them. *They come in handy sometimes.*

Their new shack was the first in a row of ten on each side of a fresh dirt patch no cars could ever access. It smelled of the earth, with minerals and clay recently overturned. The shack had three metal walls so far and no roof. Ricardo still needed to bring the rest. For now, a rough brown tarp was draped over the unfinished structure and tenuously tethered by some rope to a few stakes in the ground. A wild milieu of green bushes and bougainvillea of every shade of purple and pink covered the embankments on either side of the *rancho.* It was oddly cleaner than other parts of the *precario,* not yet littered with everyone else's trash.

Ricardo worked all yesterday to cut the packed dirt descending the hill so, at least in the mornings before the rain, they wouldn't slip. Even still, Olga worried the land above would give way. She squeezed the thought from her mind.

Empty handed, Ariel started down the dirt stairs first. Stepping onto the peat-perfumed ground, Olga passed their new neighbor across the way. A bucktoothed woman was beating a mutt out in front. His eyes bulged a deep red and his chain was nailed to the ground so he couldn't escape. The woman struck the dog again. Olga winced and turned away. The woman cackled as she retreated into her dwelling.

Another shack was slowly being constructed next to their new place. Mismatched pieces of corrugated metal and wooden planks were added little by little.

"I bet they'll finish this weekend," Olga said confidently. She didn't need to look at Ariel to sense her incredulity.

Mom was out in front. She wasn't wasting any time starting her garden again. She had lugged old rubber tires down the stairs, eventually just letting them fall off the cliff above, then walking down the stairs to roll them toward the lean-to. She laid them prone on the dirt around the metal walls. She carefully filled each tire with dirt and sunk the base of a flower in each one. Her tomato plants along the right side of the house were already taking root.

Ariel nudged the door open with her hip. Ricardo and all the boys filed in. They dropped their loads mostly in the right places. Olga's four-year-old brother Josue sat on a piece of red raggedy carpet that was meant to be installed but was instead flopped on the ground, their futon weighing down one edge. None of their wrinkled posters had been hung yet and they were still waiting for a water hook up. For now, dented jugs of water lined the far wall where the sink would eventually be. Empty buckets for gray water sat next to them.

Jose was slicing purple construction paper with dull scissors. He pressed himself up to toddling, his fingers still entwined in the handles. He teetered over to paste his creations one by one on the particle board door of their room. All uneven, rudimentary, and sticky.

"I actually like it here. I wanna buy this land someday," Ariel said as they unloaded a few bags in the living room.

"Just 170 million *colones*," Olga said, turning to leave again. Olga couldn't let her sister imagine a level of wealth like that. Not for people like them. A place they'd never reach, it was an idea that needed to be checked.

"Where're you goin'? We're not done."

"I gotta go see Cristina. Promised her I would," Olga lied.

Looking like she would rebound and want to accompany her, Ariel instead shrank in place. Josue crawled over and snatched up more paper with his gummy hands.

Olga clutched her bright pink plastic purse and applied screaming red lipstick to her puckered face through the cracked reflection in the mirror on the back of their front door.

"See you guys later," she said, walking out the open door.

Olga passed her mother in the garden.

"*¡Chao Mom!* See you!" Olga walked faster than she knew her mother's voice could travel. Xianne's maternal reminders trailed off as Olga bounded up the stairs.

CHAPTER 11

RED BANDANA

—

"All right, line up on the side of the field with your partners," the woman said.

She had tight, perm-like curls and dressed in all white with her T-shirt tucked into her waistband. She held a clipboard with a bedazzled clip that scintillated when the light hit it, and the flashes pierced Cristina's retinas from far away. The woman tossed an electric green pen around in her mouth between instructions. She talked so fast but seemed to say nothing. Cristina hoped she never looked like her.

Cristina wasn't restarting school—this was inevitable. It was too hard to keep up. Everyone in her grade was a year ahead by now. Laura, a friend she'd met in her last year, wasn't the kind to do anything on her own and had begged Cristina to go to orientation anyway. "Moral support." Of all the girls in school, she was the prettiest and didn't seem to care what other people thought. Cristina admired that.

"Wanna come with us to the park tonight near Vaqueros?" Laura said.

Half following instructions, the girls made their way across the bucolic park near the high school that ended in a terraced row of trees. It was the nicest park around. Cristina didn't tell many people where she lived, not even Laura. Other clusters of prepubescent teens started to walk with varying degrees of obedience. The girls were still taller than some boys.

"I can't. I have to watch Jacob," Cristina said.

"Nah! No way. Baby stuff? You gotta be out, livin' your life." Laura nodded to emphasize the words. "We're gonna party. You should come."

Laura seemed to know just the tone to use when abetting. Cristina's jugular felt hot. She wanted to go but couldn't. If she waited too long to respond, Laura would throw another dart.

"Hurry up everyone!" the instructor said.

With a lag, the group grumbled toward the side of the field.

"Now, make sure you have a partner. One person in each team should tie the blindfold to cover the other's eyes. Then that person will give directions, telling them where to walk."

Cristina slumped her shoulders and regretted coming. She was annoyed at herself for not mustering an excuse.

"Wanna go first?" Laura said.

"Fine." Cristina turned around to put her back to Laura.

She tied a red bandana around Cristina's head of dark, thick hair. It was a little too tight to be comfortable, but she didn't say a thing.

"All right everyone, now go!" The instructor was a little too keen.

The girls started out.

"To the right!" Laura said.

Cristina started wandering, forcing her eyelids against the bandana, trying to see through the small slit of light at the bottom of her field of vision; arms by her side, shoulders still slumped.

"No! Left!"

Cristina was startled. *Didn't she just say right?*

"Left more!"

Time slowed down behind the blindfolded.

"Okay, now speed up, you're close to the end! You can go faster!" Laura said.

Cristina quickened her legs, starting to jog, lifting her arms. All at once, her fists, then nose, struck a concrete wall. She ricocheted backwards, stumbling, trying to get her balance, and pulled off the bandana. Laura was doubled over laughing and couldn't catch her breath.

"What're you doing?" Cristina said, scrunching her face. She touched her fingers to her nose. A droplet of blood rolled down her philtrum and across her upper lip. It separated in two when it met the crease of her mouth, tracing the line of her lips encased in cheap, flaking pink lipstick.

Laura twisted her head toward the other groups that were far away. "I don't want Cristina on my team. She's so useless!" Laura said, raising her voice so they could hear.

More blood streamed from her nostrils and stained her technicolored cotton shirt—one of few she actually liked. Cristina restrained her tears, making herself nauseous instead. *I can't let her see me cry.* She stood there, stunned, with red fingers as her head started to ache.

Laura sighed with a devious smile and let her laughter taper off. She'd had her fun.

"Don't be a *carapicha* and not come to the park tonight, okay?"

A wave of shame engulfed Cristina's whole body, starting with her chest and emanating out in all directions. It moved so fast and so thick that it might've even caught up to Laura as she turned and walked away.

CHAPTER 12

THE HIGHWAY

———

Gabriela perused a large stack of bright green posters on a folding table in the shade of a Palanco tree at the top of the fire road. Neighbors started gathering. The bridge was down the hill in the distance. Gabriela counted the people as they arrived. *Five. Eight. Twelve. Sixteen. Thirty-three. Fifty-seven. Ninety.* She furrowed her brow as she struggled to name the number that came after. The crowd swelled, some people propping up umbrellas to block them from sunspots. *They'd be there awhile.*

Ricardo picked up one of the posters. "August 15 is the last day to leave. Can you believe this?"

Mamá was busy arranging the table.

Ricardo continued, staring at the paper. "It says here, 'unregistered households will not be eligible for resettlement subsidies.' And CMSSN has a number to call. How are people supposed to know what CMSSN is?"

Ricardo let the poster slide onto the table. It missed, drifting instead to the uneven road. Before it had time to settle, Gabriela picked it up, studying the text on the page. The words made no sense.

"I'm just tired. Fifteen years we've been hearing about this back and forth," Mamá said.

Gabriela peered up at her mother. The sun found its way through the leaves and stained her eyes. Gabriela blinked, trying to get the spots to go away.

"I heard there's two companies wanting to come in and build. Sounds like they're thinking about leveling Sector 1 for condos," Ricardo said.

"I don't think we can stop 'em. They knew exactly what they were doing last week with the bulldozers and the flooding. They want a highway, they want fancy condos, and that's that," Mamá said.

"They either ignore us or want us out. Like if they closed their eyes, we'd all just disappear," Ricardo said.

Gabriela didn't like to close her eyes. Sleeping was scary; taking naps was scary. Things might disappear if she did.

Mamá walked down the fire road, descended into the crowd, and greeted everyone as she went. She reappeared next to a row of shacks with a clipboard. People stood all around her. Héctor positioned a large black speaker beside her and overturned a red plastic crate, slapping his hand down on it and smiling up at Mamá.

Taking Héctor's hand, Mamá stood up on the crate. A tall man stood next to her with a shirt that read, "Development Association." He was dressed in a black leather vest with silver rivets, jeans with a large silver belt buckle, and rings on every finger. A silver watch encircled his weathered wrist. The tips of his cowboy boots curled upward and moved as he paced around the riser. The pastor stood behind her. As if everyone knew the same silent cue, all the heads bowed at once.

"May God keep us united in community in these times of trials, that he may lift us above the politics and help us carry on," the pastor said.

The crowd was placid, spellbound by his words. Mamá stood firm in her plaid pastel shirt, black hat, and skirt with her head bowed. After a long pause, Mamá started.

"The government has decided *we're* the barrier." She swallowed and clutched the microphone tighter with every word.

"There are people in the government who wanna tell me we haven't lived in extreme poverty."

The crowd let out a faint grumble that rose above the heat and the umbrellas. Mamá kept on.

"But this highway project has been in the works for four years, and we've been looking for a solution to make sure everyone who lives here has a place to go. I respect those in government trying to help and work with us. I understand they have other plans for this land: a highway meant to connect the north and south sides of the city and some condos for people who can afford it."

The calm of the prayer had worn off and now more people were standing around. Some booed.

"I understand they have a difficult job, but I've told them all people have a right to dignified shelter for their children. So, we are waiting for a coordinated solution to ensure that families here receive housing. We will not rent! We will stand for nothing less than a pathway to ownership."

The crowd fed off Mamá's energy and broke into applause. Gabriela looked around, unsure of why they were clapping. She touched her hands together slowly, joining in. More people cheered and others waved their hand fans in the air.

"I am not the community. I am merely your representative, so I need your support to be able to do my job."

Mamá began to tremble. Another woman from the crowd reached out to hand her a bottle of water. Mamá looked down and took it. Beads of water dripped down her wrist as she took two small sips and handed the bottle back to the nameless face.

"Each family has the option to mark their preference for a relocation site on the forms we will pass out," Mamá said, pointing to the paper in her hand. "If none of those locations interest you and your family, mark 'none.'"

The paper looked like the ones Fernando liked to scribble on.

"You have the right to look for your own housing if the options offered by the government don't suit you. Those who are registered within the 2012 census are eligible for subsidies from CMSSN and need to make an appointment with DNF to discuss the possibilities."

Sweaty and agitated, a small group of young men in the crowd began to shout.

"CMS . . . what? This don't make sense!" one person yelled.

"I'm not registered. What then? No options?" another said.

"*Sí*, me neither. This is a bunch of bullshit."

"They're a bunch of crooks trying to pawn off land they don't even own. You think we're gonna get those titles? No way!"

"*¡Cálmense! ¡Cálmense!* Calm down! Let her speak!" The leather-clad man yelled over the crowd.

Mamá continued. "This isn't the time to argue. Each family needs to take some responsibility! You have rights, even as immigrants, but no one is going to do it for you. I know that'll be hard for some of you."

Immigrants. That was a new word for Gabriela. She repeated it over and over in her head, just the way Mamá said it. A hand-painted sign hung above one of the churches overlooking the crowd: "Missions Impossible." The sky turned to an afternoon filled with clouds. It would rain today too.

"We have to work together on this. There's no reason to fight among ourselves, because that's exactly what everyone expects. We need to show them we're organized and united," Mamá said. A mulish few started to drift away from the margins of the crowd.

"Now, I've also been told there are 170 square meters of land being offered up in *Imperial* and another portion in Guajillo. There are proposals out there, and thanks to God, people are supporting us."

The crowd calmed down.

"Families that aren't registered by the census will need to wait until the Department of Migration and Nationality comes 'round to give you appointments to apply for subsidies."

A distant voice from the crown said, "What if we rent?"

"It doesn't matter if you rent one square meter in this place, the government wants you out."

"And by when?" another voice called out.

"August 15. We've got just less than two months."

Gabriela squatted on the porch behind the folding table, letting her little torso drape over her legs. Her armpits were perfect covers for her knees. She picked up a small stick and scraped it across the ground, leaving a brown mark. She pushed the end of the stick into her palm, fluttering her fingers over the stick: the sign language word for "leaf."

Mamá walked up the hill toward Gabriela. A few neighbors trailed behind her. The rest of the crowd milled about. Some in the middle stayed put and others dispersed.

"*Vámos mija*," Mamá said, taking Gabriela by the hand with a stack of posters in the other.

They turned down one of the slum lanes by the church. Orange barricades meant for the highway lined the pathway with weeds finding every which way to grow through them.

Gabriela squirmed and contorted her body, alternating between skipping and walking. They approached a door and Mamá knocked. They all had the same rattle to them.

A man answered the door in a tattered orange T-shirt, slackened gym shorts, socks with holes in them, and slip-ons. He hid behind the door and shifted his weight from one leg to the other. Just his face and neck were visible. People always looked so afraid when Mamá came around.

"¿Sí, señora?"

"Hi, I'm Doña Jimena, coming by to share information about the *desalojo* and what you need to do to relocate."

"Okay." The man in the doorway seemed disappointed.

"You have six options: *Guajillo, Orotepe, Sevilla, Orotina, Los Chiles,* and *Pueyrredon.*"

His disappointment gave way to obstinance.

"All those are more than six hours away! How am I supposed to keep my job?"

"I'm sorry, sir, but I'm just the messenger."

"Look," he said, pausing to lower his gaze. "We lease out several places here to neighbors. You can't just take that money away from us."

"This *desalojo* is meant to untangle the knot, not tighten it." Mamá handed him a flyer and started to walk away.

Mamá was always so straightforward. She always knew what was right, but people were angry with her no matter what. Mamá needed to play more.

Gabriela reached over and swiped two posters from her mother's hands to get her attention.

"Gabi! Stop it! Either walk with me nicely or we're done."

Gabriela whined and stomped her feet. The soles of her feet stuck to the plastic of her pink galoshes. She clutched the green paper in her hand, scrunching it up.

As they continued to the next door, Gabriela peered down another long narrow corridor. At the end she could see a dog wandering around with a chain around its neck. A scruffy old man came up behind Mamá, getting too close.

"Why'd ya only give it to my wife? *I'm* the man of the house. *I* am!" He had one of Mamá's flyers in his hand.

"*Señor,* we're giving one form to each household ,and your wife was the person at the door. Feel free to read the papers and speak with her about it."

"I was here when they started," he slurred his words, emphasizing all the wrong letters. "I think it's crazy that the government is kicking me out. Buncha *cabrones.*"

Mamá nodded without saying a word and continued to walk in the same direction they were already headed.

"I'm a founding member. Did ya hear me? Thirteen years ago and *now? Now?* I know what's goin' on here!" He strung together sentences that didn't seem to work.

Mamá faced him. "I understand your frustration, but I hope you can cooperate with us."

"But I was here at the beginning!"

Mamá put her hand on Gabriela's back and ushered her in front of her as they resumed their walk. Mamá never ran. Not for fun or even for danger.

Mamá looked down at Gabriela as they walked. *Mamá never looks at me.* The man was still yelling at them.

"*Mija,* send me to a different *precario* where I can actually get some work done," Mamá said to her with a big sigh.

What did she mean? Gabriela's heart sank. *Why not just stay here with me?*

PART III

LEAF CUTTERS

CHAPTER 13

TOLTERO

—

Armon peered through the smeary backseat window of the taxi. A group of boys in ill-fitting jerseys played on the well-tended grass among the birds-of-paradise in front of the hotel, meters from the highway's edge. The owners of the hotel had put barbed wire around the premises to keep them out, but they were nimble enough to climb and didn't seem to care about a few scratches. Armon used to play there when it was just an empty lot. No hotel, no fancy garden—the landscaping now made it more enticing than the patchy field next to the center.

The taxi slowed and came to a stop on the side of the highway near the *precario*. Armon stepped out of the unmarked taxi as highway traffic whizzed by, leaving a whirring noise in his ears.

A taller boy kicked a soccer ball missing most of its hexagons. It barreled through the air toward the highway as the other boys threw up their hands, exasperated. The ball bounced toward Armon. He swiveled his hips and let the ball ricochet off the inside of his shoe, kicking it back to them. The boys seemed to melt with relief that another ball was not lost to the highway. They were hard to come by.

Armon slammed the door closed and descended the embankment toward the *precario*. He made his way through the only passageway with access from the northwest side. It was steep and usually dotted with smoldering trash piles. It was a little different today. Too quiet.

As he rounded the corner, a small crowd was assembled. Opposite the group, a green wall of corrugated metal had nearly thirty fresh bullet holes in it. They made a perfect circle of metal bent onto itself. A few others had punctured surrounding houses. Someone was crying.

Damion was on the edge of the crowd. Armon made his way over to him, still unable to see.

"*Hermano*, what happened?" Armon said.

"Yo, it's Tolte. He's gone."

"What? I was just with him earlier."

"In broad daylight, yo. One of them *pucheros* probably tipped 'em off."

"But that makes no sense."

"I don't know, dawg, he was into somethin'."

Armon stretched his neck to see above the heads. Someone had covered Tolte's body with a light pink fringed bath towel already soaked with blood. It reeked of rotting meat. The smell of the little white flowers on orange trees rested lightly above it all. People in the crowd were crying. Other towels draped over two more belly-down figures, one with toenails painted pink. A milk carton had exploded nearby; a white circle mixed with dirt seeping into the ground. Armon had seen things like this before. Just more bodies. *But Tolte? How did that happen?*

"He got greedy," Damion said, unprompted.

Damion was probably right. It was the certainty of the cartel's movements. The *precario* boys were just peons, controllers of territory, there to do a job. This was way bigger than them. *Tolte should have known better.*

"He just couldn't wait for his cut. I bet he skimmed off the top. Impatient fuck," Damion said. He seemed to console himself with the logic that *he'd* never do anything like that. He was safe.

In that moment, they needed Jimena. Armon hadn't seen her in a while. It nagged at him like the distance with his own mother never did. She was the one hovering above all the bullshit, trying to make this place work.

"Yo, I'll catch you in a bit," Armon said as he took off jogging down the slum lane to find Jimena.

Armon ducked around the crowd, hugging the Jansport slung tightly over his shoulder. He couldn't be seen in this part. He weaved through the corridors and emerged onto the fire road, passing more neighbors crying along the way. Armon thought he was out of tears. Things like this didn't faze him anymore. A numbness. Another boss gone. It wasn't the first.

Armon tapped his round knuckles against the ligneous door. Hollow and rickety.

"¿Sí?" Her soft voice came from inside. She was trusting and never afraid to answer. Armon was always amazed by that.

"¿Doña Jimena?" he said.

"¿Sí? Who is it?" Her voice got louder as she pulled the plywood open. A little boy he hadn't met ran up beside Jimena and let out a roaring sound, extending one fist to the air. Seeing Armon, Jimena's expression drooped. *Was it fear? Disappointment?*

"What's goin' on?" Jimena said.

"Look, I dunno know how to say this, but—" Armon paused, waiting for Jimena to give him a sign.

"Well, spit it out."

"There's been another shooting."

The color fled from Jimena's rosy face and the bags under her eyes swelled. Realizing what she could be thinking, Armon added, "It wasn't me, ya know. I just came upon it now. Everyone's down there. I'm sorry, but it looks like civilians."

Jimena didn't speak. It was that power of hers he struggled with most. The unspeakable shame, knowing he was part of it all, and knowing she knew it; the inability to tear himself away from a sadness that knew no depths, from fear, from the need to survive.

Jimena turned back into the shack to grab some things, leaving the door open. She darted around her living room, looking unsure of what to take. The little boy donned a Superman costume. He sensed Jimena's distress and didn't look so mighty anymore. Armon remembered how much he wanted a superhero costume when he was small. Armon cracked a smile. *At least this little dude got one.*

Jimena grabbed an empty fishbowl still crusted with mildew at the bottom. She tucked it under her armpit, pressing it against her ribs, pulling the door closed, and leaving Superman behind.

"Show me," Jimena said.

Armon bowed his head in reverence and they walked down the few steps onto the fire road. His shoes didn't quite fit him. They felt like boats weighing him down. Armon watched Jimena notice the crowd and trudge ahead of him. She didn't say a word. *All too familiar.*

Jimena placed her arm around one of their neighbors as they crumpled over with despair. With the other hand, Jimena handed the fishbowl to another. Her underarm skin drooped with wrinkles as her bicep flexed above, holding up the glass. The man took it with both hands and held it close, digging his weathered hand into his pocket, pulling out three coins. One fell to the ground. He crouched, fumbling among feet, pinching the coin between his index and thumb, and taking a little dirt with it. Standing up, he sunk them in the fishbowl. Three faint clanks rang out among the sobs. The man hugged the jar and passed it to the next person, burying his head in his hands.

CHAPTER 14

RED

"Go ahead without me, please," Cristina said. "I'm really not feeling well." Patricia wasn't buying it. She saw through her like no one else.

"Fine, do what you want."

Cristina watched as her sister gathered her sweatshirt and a tattered script of *La Llorona*. *What a weird play to be doing.* Cristina hated theater club and was annoyed her sister was even going. She wasn't even that into it—it was just something to do to fill the seemingly endless amounts of time God had cursed them with.

Patricia opened the thin door of their room and walked out, leaving it ajar. Cristina saw into the living area, where Patricia stood talking to Ma. Little sister Belén dragged a white bucket half her size into the house and starred into it with disgust.

"Ma! Is this yours?" she said, looking down, tilting it away from herself. Something had died in there and Roger had found it.

"No! Toss it outside, *mi amor!*" Vivia didn't skip a beat.

Gross.

Why was everything always dying around here?

Kicking the door closed with her foot, Cristina fell back onto her bed and into her thoughts. The worn-out mattress didn't have any bounce anymore. She thought of how she bounced off the concrete slab. Papi's face when she confronted him. Laura and her judgmental friends. A sinking feeling, one with no way out. The mattress enveloped her. Vivia and Alonso seemed so worried. Annoying to no end.

Reaching under her mattress, she pulled out a pen with a metal tip. The sharp wire of the bed frame scratched the back of her hand. With the pen in her right, she drew on her left wrist.

"I . . . hate . . . this."

She wrote it again, this time pressing the pen tip deeper. It broke her skin and a single bead of blood collected at the surface like a rusty red balloon.

It stung.

Cristina turned over on her side, then to her stomach, and reached beneath her bed, waving her hand around in the dark. Wiggling her fingers, she sifted through the piles of stuff until she found it. Unraveling her gaunt body back to where she was, Cristina rested the cool metal blade on her chest and closed her eyes. Adrenaline filled her jawbones. She could be anywhere but here. She traced the handle across her collarbone until she found her bicep, pressing the edge into her muscle. The house noise faded into the background.

Each incision was small. She was careful not to make a mess of it. Each time the knife creased her skin, she felt better. Sadder. Numb. Cristina lined them up parallel in perfect succession.

This wasn't the first time. She had done it once before in the sixth grade and nearly everyone found out. It was their fault she didn't want to be at school and wasn't studying.

Down to the small wrinkle in the soft side of her elbow. It was all a rush—a woozy, almost happy sensation. Her heart beat faster as she continued down her arm toward her wrist. One by one. Barely remembering the best cuts of them all. Time sped up.

She heard her sister's faint, quivering voice.

"Ma!" Patricia said, running up to her bedside.

Cristina felt hot, crumpled up in the bed covers with the cool touch of blood-soaked sheets on her skin.

"Ma!"

Patricia was frantic, but Cristina was calm. She felt Patricia press herself against her body, almost for balance.

Vivia shrieked.

"Call the neighbor!"

Cristina felt a whiff of air as Patricia bolted out of wooden door.

Cristina was suspended among the hurry, where she always wanted to be. Vivia knelt by her side, sopping up the blood with a beach towel they got from Goodwill.

She felt another presence in the room.

"¿Qué pasó? What happened?" A man's voice. *Ricardo? Is that you?*

"Something happened! She's bleeding!"

She felt burly, hairy arms and hands slide under her back and legs. She felt limp and safe with nothing to do. *Where was Paps? Did he care?*

Cristina felt dizzy as someone pressed their legs into the floor to stand.

Her body bounced around in the back of a beat-up Chevy truck, cradled in her mother's arms. *It must be Ricardo.* He was the only one in their section with a car. Cristina drifted in and out of consciousness. She felt someone squeezing her arms and wrists like they didn't have enough hands to hold it all in. The blood kept coming, spilling all over the backseat.

~

Cristina awoke, still in a daze. Pieces of black thread cascaded down her arms. A translucent plastic tube filled with blood protruded from the arm with fewer cuts. *Is that mine?*

There was a low murmur in the room. Cristina hated the hospital, but it was clean. She yearned for a hygienic home. Somewhere clean, with white, fluffy towels she could bury her face in, unafraid to smell something she didn't want to. The hospital room had green concrete walls and an actual floor. *Maybe I could just move in.*

"I think the right thing to do is admit her, at least for a few days," one woman in blue scrubs said.

"I don't think it's necessary. It was just one incident and being home is probably best," another said.

Still here.

She hated how everyone treated her like an object and talked over her as if she weren't awake. *God, if you exist, don't make me stay here another day.*

A woman in scrubs leaned over her with an inquisitive look. "The first thing you need to do is pray."

Who does she think she is?

Cristina used to talk to God. Other people seemed to know him. They looked happy. She even went to church once, but the singing was stupid. How could she be in this whole mess if God really loved her like they said he did? Cristina lay there in the hospital bed motionless, wishing to be in Ricardo's arms again just for a second.

Patricia had been standing there, listening. She hadn't said a word. Vivia look tired and devastated.

"I'll be right back, *mi amor*," Vivia said.

Vivia didn't seem to want to be around her. The nurse and Vivia left the room, exposing Patricia, who was standing there slightly pigeon-toed. She waited for them to all file out and then lunged toward the bed.

"I think you *do* want to live." The words fell out of her mouth as she slid to her knees on Cristina's bedside.

Cristina let her sister's voice hang, pretending not to hear, and closed her eyes.

"I think . . . I think you're looking for some magical, easy way out that just doesn't exist. This isn't the way, Tina," she said, gaining confidence. "I think you would've done it differently if you really wanted out."

CHAPTER 15

PÁJAROS

Mamá had forgotten to cover the canary's cage before she left. It was perched near their front door. Mamá adored her birds, but today she winced at the chatter. In another blue, rusted cage next to the canary's, the two lovebirds sat wing to wing on a single rung. They didn't have any toys like Gabriela had, but they were just birds anyway, and they had each other. Mamá kept the parakeets farther away in a third cage to avoid the cacophony that made even their most patient neighbors complain.

Today it didn't matter. Everyone was fussy.

Keeping a reasonable distance, Gabriela sat in a squat beneath the hanging cages where she watched their little heads move in sudden motions. White poop spattered in tie dye patterns on the floor. Mamá had said not to play with it; instead, she squinted her eyes to make it into different shapes like clouds.

Not looking where it was headed, Mamá tossed a tattered rag over the cage, covering only half as it landed. It smelled a little like Ricardo's car: oily, grungy, and comforting. Below it, the canary puffed his spotted neck feathers in theatrical display then bobbed his head in submission. Fernando was glued to the TV nearby.

Mamá had just sat at the table when Vivia's big brown eye peered through the slit in the door. Her sandal inched it ajar, and soon she was standing in their living room.

"*Señora*," Vivia said, trying to hide her eagerness. Mamá looked up at her visitor.

"*Páse*, come in," Mamá said.

Vivia sat down at the table covered with a plastic white-and yellow-checkered cloth with painted cherries that all looked the same. A few green flyers remained.

"*Señora*, can I ask a few questions?" Vivia said, settling in. "With the *desalojo*, I don't have a *cédula*, an ID card. What should I do?"

"I hate to say it, but you have to get one. They're not approving families for subsidies unless they're documented. They're starting with people on the census roster from five years ago, then going on to people that just got them now."

Vivia suctioned her tongue against the roof of her mouth, letting out an indignant click and narrowing her eyes.

"It's 18,000 *colones* every month for insurance for each of my girls, *and* they need their insurance cards before they can get their *cédula*." Vivia let a big burst of air leave her cheeks. "I have no idea how I'm gonna to pay for all that."

"Are you working right now?"

"I can't clean houses with all the *chiquillos* all by myself. I'd only make 500 *colones* an hour and 25,000 *colones* every two weeks. Nowhere near enough. No point in paying for the bus and babysitting. We have to eat first, *sabe*?"

Tiny animal trinkets arranged on shelves stared down at Gabriela as she half listened to the big people's gibberish.

"I know it's tough, but you just have to do it." Mamá seemed to be out of consolations. Mamá shifted her attention to the television, which had been on for as long as Gabriela could remember. It was incessant and too colorful for Gabriela to focus on.

"Turn off the TV, *mi amor!*" Mamá said.

Ripples in Fernando's pilled nylon Spiderman costume appeared as he slumped at the suggestion. He lifted his chin toward Mamá and whined, dropping his arms by his sides in inconsequential resistance. *Even though Mamá isn't his real Mamá, he must know by now that he'll never win with her.*

"*¡Ahora!* Now, please!"

Fernando lumbered over to the television, sticking his little index finger in the slot where the off-kilter power button was. He plopped his small bottom into the plastic rocking chair in the corner. It was just his size. Mamá's tired smile emerged for a moment. Fernando was fighting the only barrier he probably knew. Vivia's anxiety demanded Mamá's attention.

"You say we have all these rights, hmm? How am I supposed to use them if it doesn't even make sense to have a job?" Vivia tapped her long, fake nails on the table with metronomic efficiency. Gabriela watched each motion as her fingers, curly and freakish, rose and fell in a dull, muted rhythm.

"I know. I get it," Mamá said, resting the side of her hand on the table and squared her legs and shoulders toward Vivia.

"First thing: focus on getting the girls insurance. Borrow money if you have to. Apply for your ID. I know it's a long line, but just bite the bullet. Register with the housing authority and then visit the state mortgage bank and apply for the subsidy. There isn't much time, so, you know, get to it."

Vivia rolled her eyes and slapped the table, her palm sticking to the plastic cloth as she lifted it.

Unable to withstand the boredom, Fernando picked up a handheld game console that didn't work and pressed the controls in his lap with erratic determination: a fledgling learning to cope.

"No one wants to talk about how unsafe this place is. Drug dealers around. People stealing things all the time. Someone even broke into Carmen's house and stole her television. Who steals a television from a *precario*?" Vivia said, standing up, turning her body toward the door as abruptly as she entered. "And there's no reason to report it because the police don't give a shit! Why would I even wanna be a citizen?"

While Vivia went on and on, Mamá stood and collected the remaining flyers on the table and positioned them in a nice, neat stack. Gabriela stood up and poked her finger in the bottom of the birdcage. Intrigued, the canary wandered over and nibbled at it.

"I know it's frustrating, but the difference between people who make it and people who don't is standing right here." Mamá motioned her palm between her and Vivia, shrugging her shoulders. "Do what you need to do."

Mamá walked over to the lovebirds' cage, towering over Gabriela. Vivia waited for what she would say. The birds scuttled their claws in the wood shavings at the bottom of the cage. They seemed nervous, as if they knew they were on display. Their susurrations filled the silence.

"Did you know that bird parents feed their children by chewing food in their beak before spitting it into the little ones' mouths?" Mamá said.

Gross.

Vivia scrunched her nose and her lips up.

"Do you know why they do this?" Mamá said.

Vivia shook her head. Curiosity dissolved her frustration for just a moment.

"Over time, the chicks eat germs the parents pick up outside the nest. Makes their babies' immune system stronger every time they eat," Mamá said.

Vivia tensed her chin muscles, pressing her lips together in understanding.

"Your kiddos are watching. Do the right thing."

CHAPTER 16

FRINGE

———

Young men poured in from Remolado and Vaqueros, two *precarios* from the other side of Monte Verde. Tattooed faces lined up on the fire road in overworn black T-shirts half-tucked in with their jeans sagging on their pelvises. A few had mustered black suits to wear. They waited to enter the small makeshift church to pay their respects. Armon and Damion stood in line on the two stairs leading up to the improvised church. It was one of the biggest wakes they'd had this year.

"So, when does Tolte's younger brother start?" Damion said, sticking his hands in his pockets.

"In three days," Armon said as the line inched forward. "No jobs until then."

"Why?"

"Maybe just so we don't lose more than one in a week?"

"It's just the churn."

"Cost of doin' business, yo. Do you think he'll be any good?"

They stepped inside the church. Flimsy white plastic folding chairs were lined up on either side of the gray tile floor. Plug-in fans with dust trails flowing behind them had been scattered about, pushing air around and not cooling anything. Smokey chipotle mixed with Lizano flavor drifted in through the barred squares in the wall where windows should've been. Armon recognized a few others in line with solemn and modest faces.

As they approached, Armon swerved his head among the people standing around, noticing the details of the coffin. It was plain but respectable, coated in a dark brown matte stain. The corners were rounded, and the edges had indents, showing that at least someone cared. Not ornate, just to the point—like Tolte. The gang didn't have much to contribute these days, so Jimena's collection covered most of it. She was one of the few who felt death was neutral territory, maybe even grounds for forgiveness. Most others were still angry and would stay that way.

Armon neared the wooden box. It lilted to one side, propped up on two uneven plastic chairs. A closed casket only meant one thing, but having not seen the face beneath the towel that day, doubt crept in. *Maybe he wasn't inside. Maybe this was all just a ruse. Maybe it wasn't Tolte that day. Maybe they staged the whole thing to steal the latest package and cover up Tolte's escape. What would that mean for me? Was I next?* Armon's fingertips traced the indentations along the edge. He wanted to lift the lid.

Armon dug into his pocket, feeling around for his plastic rosary. Armon didn't pray much and didn't really know how, but if there were ever a moment to use a rosary, now seemed appropriate. His grandfather had taught him the meaning of the beads, the difference between the ovals and the larger round ones with faces on them, but Armon had been too young to remember. The plastic felt rough under his thumb and index finger.

He steadied himself on one of the chairs that wobbled beneath his weight. He knelt down on one knee, clutching the rosary, and lowered his head in reverence. He thought he looked the part. He lifted his eyes to try peering into the crack in the coffin. *Was it really him? Or had Tolte just met the morgue rule—in the gang 'til death?*

Staring into the crack of this coffin, Armon's mind flashed to when he was thirteen and shot someone for the first time. He had panicked and didn't know where to go. The first place he had thought of was a church, just blocks from rival territory. The pastor had recognized him and told him to leave right away, saying he would pray for him, but Armon couldn't stick around. The rejection had been painful and dug deep into his heart. He'd made a mistake, but surely a priest could see that. He had wanted them to kill him right then and there; instead, he had snatched a Bible from the pew and left the church crazed. It had been the very next book he learned to read after the magazines. He had marched toward the *salon* of the *clika* he belonged to, mustering the courage to say he wanted out.

"C'mon dawg, yous takin' foreva. Any day now," Damion said, interrupting his thought.

Armon turned his head and smirked at him with momentary annoyance, catching in his periphery the long line behind him. *Couldn't Damion see he was doing something important— getting information that would help them stay alive? If they could reach Tolte, the most powerful of the* clika, *then what was stopping the top dawgs from killing them, too?*

"Fine. Your turn," Armon said, lifting himself to standing and pivoting to make his way back down the made-up aisle. He mopped the sweat from his chin. It felt strange to be standing at the altar at the front of a church; it was a view he never got to experience. *Did priests ever get used to that?*

As he walked down the rows of chairs, deferential and quiet, a hooded figure sat hunched in the last row. He glanced up at Armon as he passed, leaving him with the imperceptible feeling that he'd been watching.

CHAPTER 17

GIRL

———

The music changed like the knob on an old radio every few lean-tos that Olga passed. A Don Omar song, *bachata,* electronic with misogynistic lyrics she had little patience for, a neighbor yelling at her colicky infant as ads spewed from the television—the different channels of their neighborhood she'd learned to ignore. Two incessant little boys trailed behind her jumping up and down.

"Head!" one said.

"Foot!" the other yelled louder.

"Arm! Brain!"

They were parts of the body she had taught them in English the week before; the few words she herself knew in another language.

Getting no rise from their audience, they changed tack. The smaller one ran ahead, holding his hands together in the shape of a gun, shrieking, "This is a stickup! A robbery!"

"No, you di'n't!"

Self-deputizing, the other ran forward, pulling him backwards by his T-shirt. Defiant, the bandit lurched forward. His threadbare shirt pressed up against his chest, revealing the concave shape of his stomach.

"This is private security! You betta let me go!" In one swift motion, the boy turned, getting his shirt twisted and stretched as he yanked himself free.

Paying them little attention, Olga turned the corner and stood in front of Cristina's house. Their front patio area opened toward a pool of green and black sewage that flowed all day with the constant burble of muck. Their sink was located outside, and it filled with water every day when it rained. Piles of wooden slats and picked-over food were stuffed in the corners of the patio area like chum. The sheets of corrugated tin barely held back the weight of the house next door.

"*Ooope!*" she said instead of knocking. She swatted away mosquitos.

Doña Vivia peered out, wearing a faded brown dress. Her restive smile revealed two silver crowns on her front teeth, and she motioned for Olga to ascend the wooden stairs stacked on the side of their house. A bare-chested man Olga guessed to be Cristina's uncle eyed her and retreated to the back room, lascivious and meek.

Olga walked gingerly up the rickety stairs to Cristina's parents' room. The baby kicked, stopping her for a moment. The television fuzz covered the din of their neighbor's music next door, creating dissonance harder to tune out than when she was channel surfing. When the volume reached a breaking point, people threw rocks on each other's roofs. The projectiles doubled as off-buttons, but they only worked half the time. Silence was rarely an option.

Olga elbowed open the side door that towered over the hillside. Cristina sat motionless on the bed, fiddling with a plush toy similar to something from a McDonald's Happy Meal. Olga wanted to cry then and there but held in for a few more moments.

"Hey, what's goin' on?" Olga said, clearing her voice as she closed the side door. She sat down on the bed, sidling up to Cristina's hunched figure. She had bandages all up and down her arm, forming a faux cast.

"Not much," Cristina paused.

One of the eyes came loose on the toy she was holding. It fell to the wooden floor, nearly falling between the cracks where the light from an orange work lantern shone through.

"What's up with your arm?" Olga motioned to her arm and almost touched it. Cristina recoiled and furrowed her brow.

"Nothing! It's just nothing."

Olga cracked a smile, unsure of how to react. *Were those cuts all sown up? Did it happen again?* Cristina wasn't following along. Olga changed her expression, fishing for what to say next.

"Babe, I'm pregnant," Olga said. It was a momentary admonition that might show Cristina it was okay to share.

Cristina entire face lit up. She seemed relieved that Olga had changed the subject.

"*¡Tuani!* That's so exciting! Aren't you excited?" Cristina said. She turned and jumped onto the bed, landing on both knees as it bounced both of them.

"I mean, it's whatever." Olga rolled her eyes, proving mostly to herself that she still had a few more weeks of being a teenager. "Mom doesn't know," Olga added, staring at her hands wrapped beneath her growing belly.

"What! *Nena,* if I were you, I'd tell right away. I'd be so scared," Cristina said.

"Everything hurts. My hips. My stomach. I'm so dizzy and I have to pretend I'm sick all the time."

"You really need to tell someone. You can't go on like this forever. Baby's coming out at some point!"

"I'm not ready. Lil' bro is still in diapers and Mom would have kittens if she knew."

"You're already so caring. You'll be fine. Look." Cristina arched her back to push her stomach out. "I have a pouch for a stomach, too!"

Olga smiled. Her breasts had started to excrete what she thought was milk.

"How's the move?" Cristina said.

"It's fine. Still happening. I escaped. It's only temporary though."

"Are you guys looking for a new house now?"

"Mm, not sure. Some guy offered us a plot of land in the city, but there's lots to work out. What about you?"

"I dunno. Ma said something about getting some government money to buy, but I just don't see it happening."

"Yeah, I feel you. Dad has his name on our new house. He used to have this tailoring business he ran out of our living room and two of my cousins worked for him. They stole from him all the time, though. Dad never had it in him to fire them. We lost so much."

"Yo, so real. My dad's exactly the same. Literally gambles away every penny. You saw him!"

"Yeah, within like two weeks, Pepe lost the cell phone I got for him and he was so embarrassed to tell me. I'm like, if Dad can't even handle a *freakin'* cell phone, how is he allowed to own our whole house?"

"Oh my god, it's so true. We could go live with Dad's family. They're always so pissy with us but we never know why. It should be the other way around with the hell he's put us through."

Olga felt the baby kick her abdomen, subtle and sweet.

"Cristi!" Vivia's voice echoed against the fragile walls of the house.

"¿Sí, Ma?" Cristina said, raising her voice to be heard through the plywood.

"Can you come here? I need your help with somethin'!" Cristina dropped her head, glaring at Olga as if she were her mother. She waited a few beats to reply.

"Coming!"

"*Dale pues,* I'll see ya later," Olga said.

"Let me know how it goes, telling your mom and all."

"Psh, yeah right!" Olga wobbled off the bed to leave. She closed the door behind her and balanced carefully against the wooden railing descending the stairs.

Out of the corner of her eye, Olga saw the little boys again. One was pushing the other against the wood paneling of a house, with his hands around the other's neck. Letting go, the smaller one began to cry, wincing his facial muscles as his mouth opened, pulling his tears down into his chest, and not taking a breath to let the sound out.

Olga passed the boy as he stood alone. His pain melted into anger and then revenge. Two teenage boys and four others sat slumped back on a makeshift bench nearby like spectators at a ball game. With a tear-strewn face, the little boy picked up a broken piece of concrete with both hands and slung it back behind his shoulders, getting the leverage he needed in order to throw it. The weight of the block almost knocked him off balance before he chucked it at them.

The group dodged the concrete piece with ease and snickered as the boy's small body flailed around. With sarcastic acquiescence, one of the older ones walked over and wove his arms under his armpits and behind his head until he was strung out like a scarecrow. His little feet barely touched the ground. Inconsolable frustration palpitated through his veins.

The boy wiggled himself loose from the neck grip and took off running down the muddy corridor. The bigger one treaded close behind, now also wielding pieces of concrete too big for his hands.

Olga walked in their direction. She turned the corner between the colorful makeshift quarters. The boys had been met by Jimena at the dead end of the pathway. They were both crying, concrete relinquished to the ground beside them.

"Go, both of you! Same room, now!" Jimena said. The two boys slouched over themselves, still crying, and walked back toward home.

Another young boy wrestled with a bitch by Jimena's side. He used his little hands to clamp down on her jaw, and the dog backed up, agitated, hitting Jimena's legs, growling, unable to shake free.

"Aye! Careful! She might bite you," Jimena said.

Jimena was revered around here. She took care of so many children that weren't hers. Where did she get all that energy?

The jacarandas bloomed into neat purple clusters. Olga passed by twin baby girls dressed in clean, matching orange and white onesies, each holding their mother's hands, and smiling faintly as they crossed the narrow concrete pathway.

At that moment, Olga wished for nothing more than to be having a girl. A sweet, small baby girl who would grow to be feisty and strong and able to tell the boys exactly what to do—just like Jimena.

CHAPTER 18

HUNDRED

———

In and out of sleep, Armon rolled around on his bare mattress with a loose sheet tangled between his legs. Images of the corpses lying motionless swirled in his head. He wrestled with the memories of being with Toltero. The cicadas had stopped. It was the quietest, most torturous point in the night.

Bang!

A loud thud shook the metal roof. The Guanacaste trees were shedding their rigid seed pods; it was that season. Armon turned over, curling the sheet into his chest, and let out a tired sigh.

Bang!

This one was louder. Too big to be a tree pod. It emanated through the walls and the reverb stopped just after reminding Armon of how precarious his shack was. The neighborhood kids were keeping everyone up for their own fun with rocks and whatever else they could find. Armon was at once exhausted and unable to sleep. The space behind his eyes burned as his stomach turned over with the nausea only early morning brings. He couldn't be bothered to set them straight.

Bang!

A third one. Armon threw the sheet off, flexing his stomach muscles to bring himself seated on the edge of the bed as it creaked. He waited in silence, rubbing the crust from his eyelids, heart now pounding with frustration he wanted to aim anywhere but at his own thoughts, taunting him and keeping him awake. He stood up, shuffling his wide feet across the tile floor, then the dirt hallway, and made his way to the front door. The rooster out back was mercifully quiet.

Armon unwrapped the chain holding the tin to the threshold and poked his head out into the night.

"Would you keep it the *fuck* down out there?"

A figured leaning against his hut turned toward him, meeting him eye to eye. Armon couldn't make out his features.

"Good to see you, too," the hushed voice said. His chest imploded. Cortisol flowed to the pit it created. Armon regretted not bringing his blade. Too sleepy to remember. Three knocks on the roof—he should've known.

"Come with me," the voice said.

Without a choice, Armon slithered his muscular arm from around the door, closing it behind him. His heart was racing out of his ribbed white shirt.

"What's this about?"

The dark figure didn't answer; he just motioned his two fingers to follow. Armon's underfoot stuck to the damp ground, trying to keep up. He traced the figure's footsteps as they headed toward the bend in the passageway where the bodies were just taken away. The figure stopped. He was thin with a hood concealing his face.

"You see what happened here?"

"No. I wasn't around." Armon tried containing his stutter.

"I said, you see what happened here?" The voice was calm and measured.

Armon understood now. "Yeah."

"One of your guys got greedy, and we don't take that lightly."

Armon nodded. The hooded statue couldn't even see him. The figure seemed to know where to walk despite the pitch black. He didn't need to see to intimidate.

"A shame we had to take the others with him. You got kids?" The stark contrast of his supposition made Armon ache.

"Uh, no, no kids. That I know of."

The shadow let out a short humming sound. He sounded irked. He brushed his foot over where the milk had spilled, scraping the rubber of his shoe against the dirt. The moon wasn't quite waning or waxing, but a strange in-between that cast a murky light on their conversation.

"This guy had a job to do that he didn't finish. I'm told you're new but capable. Would you agree?"

"Y—yeah, I've done a few routes. Francisco to Matadero, Huaco to Jalisco and back. Usually a kilo at a time, nighttime runs, by myself or with a few others." Armon ran through his mental list of cities, trying to think of the most mountainous, challenging routes he'd done.

"Good. Then you won't be bothered carrying our next hundred."

Armon was stunned. His jaw went loose as he calculated how many runs that would be.

All the cocaine came from Colombia. He could fit five kilos in his small black Jansport backpack and dart through the night with two or three other *corredores. But a hundred?*

Sometimes they'd travel the routes by car. They called it *la carnada.* A motorcycle would ride two kilometers ahead, checking for police, and the bait motorcycle would warm the car driver to either reroute or turn off the road. If the police knew this trick, they'd have to pay them off. Where would he get the money to do it? The same police officers that stopped them on the road would arrive at the warehouse each week to collect their *tajada*—cut of the earnings. *A hundred?* How would he do it? He couldn't be the right person for the job. There had to be someone else.

"You tell no one. Not even the other *corredores.*"

"All due respect," Armon had heard that in American movies and thought it appropriate for the moment, "but that could take months."

"You do this job alone, you hear me? New crop of police around here, they're not easily bought off, so we gotta keep it under the radar."

"Okay," Armon said with an uptick.

"We need it there in no more than thirty days. Big order from down south, and we hear this place is about to go. I'm sure you understand."

"I . . ." Armon didn't have a rebuttal. It was a rare moment of intimidation. Something about this figure, something about the woman lying prone, just out to get milk probably for her kids, something about the color of the moonlight just then. His feet were getting cold.

"We'll drop it all in the back of your place next week," the figure paused, "oh, and next time, answer me on the first knock."

The figure turned and walked up the hill into the great expanse of tiny huts, still quiet and dim. Armon exhaled.

Of the seventy *corredores* he had started with, only a few had gotten out. One now worked for a new Chinese electricity company and another at a chicken joint doing twelve-hour shifts. The rest were either dead, in jail, or still running. This had the stirrings of something that could either catapult him to the top of the ranks or be a fatal mistake. It needed to be foolproof: something that wouldn't compromise him or make him go it alone. Armon wracked the recesses of his mind for ideas of anything he could cobble together.

They couldn't be serious about doing this job alone. It was just too big. He was a resourceful guy—they knew that. Armon had heard of a family that had just moved. Their father was a drunk and he knew they needed the cash. They'd be his first stop in the morning.

As Armon teetered back to his shack now fully awake and plotting, the cicadas had started singing again. Some people hated their buzzing, but he found it rhythmic and soothing, their constant presence a reminder that God might save him, whatever he had to do.

PART IV

LA MARABUNTA

CHAPTER 19

CLEAR

—

Olga was sitting on a wooden pallet her mother had fashioned for a porch. Mom had both feet firmly planted in her improvised garden in front of their house just a few paces away. She stood among the plants a little awkwardly in soiled gardening gloves. Vivia sat facing her in a squeaky metal rocking chair Mom found abandoned down by the bridge the other day. She made Olga drag it all the way here and down the stairs.

"Did you hear that fire fight a few days ago?" Mom said, crouching down in the dirt again.

"They were shootin' forever! I ran to the back of my room, farthest from the street. *Los chiquillos* and I took cover. Belén cried through the whole thing," Vivia said, steadying her voice to sound light and unemotional. She seemed to try to believe they hadn't been in danger.

"It's the cartel, *sabes?* Running up against these local guys. Once they get going, it's bad news," Vivia said.

"Don't say that out loud," Mom said, standing up. She leaned over and put her hands over Olga's ears to pantomime earmuffs. It was abrupt and unnecessary.

"Mom!" Olga said, brushing her mother's hands from her head as if swatting at flies.

"Yeah, it's all the local guys, too," Vivia lowered her voice slightly in deference.

"The poor woman. I heard she was just out to get milk," Olga added.

"It's a shame," Viva said and grabbed the rusted edges of the rocking chair to steady herself as she stood. "Well, at least you're settling in now, whether the police telling you to move were real or just another one of the city's tricks."

Olga had suspected the same thing. First the eviction order, then the flood. It didn't make things any better for Mom. Vivia looked a little ashamed she'd even said it.

"I should go. Good to see you ladies," Vivia said, lowering her head. Olga was a "lady" now. That was a step up.

"*Bueno.* Good to see you. Give your darlings a big hug for me," Mom said.

Vivia gathered up her excuse to come over and gossip— Xianne's borrowed yellow pan—and walked slowly across the rancho toward the staircase of death. No one had fallen off yet.

As Mom turned to go inside, Olga stopped her.

"Mom?"

"*¿Sí, mi amor?*"

"I . . ." Olga started to speak. "I have somethin' I gotta tell you."

"I'm listening." Xianne glanced up to see if Vivia was still in earshot. Olga heard the gate clank.

"I'm . . ." Time slowed down. The cicadas began to hum. Olga had never heard them so clear.

"I'm pregnant."

There.

She said it.

Finally.

Like a grown-ass adult.

Mom let out a breath and quickly inhaled, as if she were expecting words to come out instead. At first her face looked crisscrossed and then her bottom eye lids turned ruby red. A single tear stretched the length of her oblong cheek.

"That's—" Mom mustered the words. "That's wonderful!" She extended her arms toward Olga. At once, Olga felt like a child again. Buried in her mother's bosom, voluptuous and comforting. It could allay her deepest sorrows and her greatest fears of whether she was ready. It didn't matter in that moment. For once, her mother was a mother.

As the two held their embrace for longer than usual, the gate on the hill above them clanked again. They left it unlocked most times now. Amid the vegetation, a stout figure in ill-fitting washed-out jeans and a T-shirt rustled through.

Mom pulled back and clutched both of Olga's arms in her hands, looking her straight in the eyes.

"He's back," Mom said in a hushed tone. The consolation of the moment fled from her face.

CHAPTER 20

THE PRAYER

———

Cristina had five different pills to take: one to sleep, one to stimulate her appetite, one to stabilize her mood, and the other two? She wasn't sure. Cristina had what felt like an endless list of doctors' appointments to attend over the next month. This was the cost of going home. Always a negotiation. *Visiting the doctor was the worst.* She would ask her how she'd been that month. *Obviously not well. Next question.* The doctor would write some notes, give her another prescription for pills she didn't want to take, and let her go. Around and around the monopoly board she went, finding ways to pass "Go" every time. This was her special skill.

Her whole family sat around the windowless living room, spellbound by her every gesture. *What would Cristina do next?* She couldn't take the awkwardness, the tiptoeing around, the edginess of it all. It was all booby-trapped.

"Everyone just needs to relax!" Cristina said.

Vivia shifted in her chair, looking away for a moment. Patricia was the only one who looked at her with any sense of normalcy ever since the accident. Cristina got up and removed the dusty sheet covering the television. The bandages up her arms crinkled as she futzed with the buttons. She turned it to

The Simpsons, dubbed with high-pitched voices spewing some semblance of Spanish. Colors flickered across the cracked screen showing only two-thirds of the picture.

A timid tap at their front door rattled the wall. Vivia planted her hands against the armrests of her chair, tipping back to build up the necessary momentum to stand. She shuffled to the door and pushed aside the row of clothes hanging from a metal pipe attached to nowhere.

"Who is it?" Vivia said.

"We're here from Saint Martin's?" The voice answered a question with a question and an uptick as their response trailed off.

Vivia opened the door just wide enough for one person to squeeze through. The draft brought with it the stagnant smell of their entryway, still piled high with trash.

"May we come in?"

One by one, they eased their way into the house with a whiff of fake humility that bothered Cristina. One even bowed to greet her. Vivia let it happen. Cristina counted. Seven people piled into their living room. Two sat down on plastic chairs placed side by side in the kitchen. There weren't enough chairs for everyone, so the rest stood, out of place. The refrigerator that made clown car noises was propped up from the dirt on a wooden pallet meant for a forklift. A stray calico cat scurried along the rafters, peering down with suspicion.

Vivia closed the door behind them and shooed Belén with her hand, indicating she should retreat to the back bedroom. In the presence of all these taller, fair-skinned people, Vivia was unassertive, even in her own home.

Cristina didn't miss a beat.

"*¿Hola?*" she said in her teenage tone.

"We're here from Saint Martin's Church. We heard about you and thought our prayer group could help. We've come so God can work through us and hopefully reach you, too."

Roger wandered out of his Styrofoam crate. The dog had tufts of hair on his paws, tail, and face, speckled with fleas. Seeing the opportunity, Cristina jumped out of the circle formed around her on its own in the living room, picking up a bottle of apple-scented Febreze, brandishing it in his direction.

"Git! Git!" She sprayed Roger in the face as he retreated to a corner.

"I thought we could all pray together," one from the church group said. He had white, desiccated skin, almost pink, and gray hair that fizzled at the ends. He seemed to be talking in Cristina's direction, coaxing her back in.

"Stay!" she said as the dog blinked and nodded his head to clear his nose. "Stupid dog." Cristina had anywhere to be but in the living room.

"*Ah bueno,* that would be nice," Vivia said across the room, their newfound disciples towering over her. "Cristina!" her mother said.

The ones who had sat down stood up and started to gather the rest. Patricia was with them, looking uncertain. They all stared back at Cristina as Roger cowered. Cristina felt the same tug as when Laura tried to get her to do something she didn't want to. They were all too sinister for her and they beamed with sympathy. She felt them hacking away at her without even moving. They did it with their eyes. The chainsaw of a devotee was no match for her cut-up insides—as if there were anything left to fell.

Cristina stood in the circle, feigning diligence. Vivia seemed satisfied with the simple act of compliance on display for the visitors. She could rarely rouse the children on her own. It only took a church mob to get there. A woman and a man Cristina didn't know picked up each of her hands without asking, as if synchronized by some master Pooh-Bah. His were pudgy, hers were boney. The gray-hair started to speak.

All of them closed their eyes and tilted their faces toward the low-hanging rafters. Cristina closed hers, quickly opening them, peering across the circle to try to catch Patricia's glance. *Not looking.* She closed hers again and reopened them, waiting to be commanded into a concrete wall again. *What is happening? Why did Ma let these people in?* Her intransigence turned to childlike curiosity. *Adults do weird things like stand in circles and chant.*

"Lord heavenly Father, we hope you cleanse the wounds of the wicked that has befallen this house. Rid it of your worst wishes, offering forgiveness and lightheartedness for any wrongs done."

Roger was also rapt, meandering back to the group. When she next opened her eyes, Cristina spotted him, released her hands from the circle, picked up the Febreze she hadn't let go far, and puffed him in the face again. The laypeople groped for her hand as she squatted on the edge of the circle, all the while trying to keep their eyes closed.

"Lord, we ask that you enrapture this household, giving them solace and peace." They all hummed along in blissful reverence, consoling themselves all the while.

After the third contrived interruption, Cristina's proverbial patience had waned. In a huff, she broke from the circle and disappeared into the entryway, emerging with a nylon cord. She tied the rope around Roger's neck, affixing the other end to a piece of metal protruding from the pile of Styrofoam where he was supposed to sit.

The chanting finally ended; everyone stood silent around the single light bulb frosted with spiderwebs hanging from the roof.

Cristina didn't feel any different after the prayer session. They all still looked so concerned. *I didn't fit in their little box.* Just as uninvited as they had come, they left.

Cristina eked out a goodbye. Intoxicated by air freshener, Roger barely flinched as they walked back through the entry area.

As the last few filed out of the house, Cristina overhead one of them say to another, "What was the name of the girl who lives here?"

A question that validated her every evasion tactic. They didn't even know who they were praying for. Cristina felt in that moment further from God than ever before, indignant and content with the chasm. She had survived again but wasn't sure when the next time would be. God didn't even know.

Cristina let herself fall backward onto their wooden bench and pulled her phone out of her pocket. She flipped through photos of her crush standing in front of a mirror, lanky and shirtless with a backward baseball cap and a long chain around his neck. Messages chirped upon receipt.

The house fell silent. Her mother had nothing to say to her, looking embarrassed at how little she controlled who came and who went. No demons lost or found, no gods returned or retreating, just as helpless as before.

CHAPTER 21

THE BEACH

Gabriela sat with her legs splayed out in a Z-shape on the blue tile floor, with one leg bent in front and the other in the back. Her body doubled over her thigh as she looked down. She liked how it was cool and flat, not like at home, with its little ridges where the rough, sandy grout met the slick surface that looked like water. She ran her fingers back and forth over it, imagining for a moment that she was at the beach. She had been there once before, the sensation of her calloused feet against the sand that seemed limitless, like she could dig forever and never reach the bottom. The waves, unpredictable and huge, bigger than her, bigger than everybody.

The center was one big cold room with a rounded ceiling in the tallest building Gabriela had ever been in. The walls were painted a shade of green halfway between the Pineapple Top crayon and Mamá's posters that made the room dark, except for the stale evening light peering in through the door. A few rudimentary decorations were taped to the vast, empty walls. Mamá and Ricardo were setting up near the door.

"The journalists write whatever they want about this place. They don't care how it comes off," Ricardo said, jabbing his finger into the newspaper on the rickety table.

The flaky ink left the words in perfect symmetry imprinted on his finger. He rubbed his index and thumb together as the dusty newsprint balled up from his sweat and drifted to the floor.

"You shouldn't read those articles. They don't know us and never talk about all the good we're doing here," Mamá said.

Ricardo was too frenetic to listen to Mamá, unlike his usual calm demeanor.

Mamá had told her the story a thousand times. As a teenager, she watched an entire cluster of huts burn to the ground. Two children died. From then on, Mamá vowed to do whatever it took to get out of the *precario* and not struggle like *abuela* struggled. *Maybe struggle was just in her bones.*

Abuela had slept in the streets of Granada most nights and asked a friend or stranger for space in a guest room for the others. She had Mamá as a teenager, moving from street corner to street corner. *Abuela* would tell Mamá how she grew heavier every week. Mamá wanted all children to be safe, fed, and educated.

Gabriela almost knew it by heart.

"*Hola,* welcome everyone," Mamá said, hugging each person who came through the metal door.

Mamá had been dragging her to these boring meetings for years. They started in their living room before the center existed. She liked the people there, though. They were different. They planned and wrote things down. They knew what they were doing.

Three people wandered in and sat around a folding table in the middle of the room. Papers and clipboards all over the table made it official.

"All right," Mamá said, standing over them and balancing her hands on the table.

They all bowed their heads at once. Mamá intertwined her fingers and let her clasped hands drop.

"God, please watch over us as we work to save our community," Mamá paused, as if she didn't know where to go with it, "In God's name, we pray, amen."

Everyone except Mamá looked around at each other, jolted by the abrupt end to the prayer.

Mamá moved on.

"Tonight, I wanted to start with a story, because I know sometimes it's hard to think back to where we came from. I remember a time when this building was the largest bar and dance hall around. Close to the bus stop, off the main road. Dirt floors, no windows, perfect for parties and prostitutes."

Gabriela was delighted by how all the sounds lined up as Mamá talked. Mamá always had a way with words.

"We turned it around. We were the ones to ask Human Services to renovate it. To make it what it is today. It took years, so let's not give it all up without a fight."

"*Querida Jimena*," an older woman spoke. "Thank you dearest. It's true. We had to fight for water and electricity. We've accomplished a lot over the years, and our *barrio* is growing."

The woman's stature was hearty and overworked. Her back was rounded at the top, and she had a tired face. Grease stained her shirt. She was the woman from the *soda* that sold the most delicious *nacatamales*.

Just like Mamá had with Fernando, she had taken in a neighbor's child several months ago when their mother went north. It was supposed to be a short trip, but the child was still with her and played at the *soda* while she worked.

"Layla, that's right. We got pipes and wires installed, what was that?" Ricardo said, glancing sideways up at the ceiling, "ten years ago? Others in the community sat back and watched."

"We founded this place. Plenty of people avoided the costs, but I paid a 170,000 *colones* for my plot of land, fair and square. Sick of war, sick of not having jobs, homes washed away by storms," Mamá said.

Ricardo interrupted her. "When no one else would, we stepped forward to organize this place into sectors, all for the government. Hand-delivering electricity bills to all five hundred-odd houses on foot and collecting the money." Ricardo was getting excited. "You know how many times I was almost robbed? How ungrateful people have been. And yet, here we are, saving them when the city comes and floods the whole place!"

Another man, Héctor, sat cross-legged at the table. He was effeminate and sharp. He kept his nails long and painted and wore a cross around his neck that protruded from his tight black tank top. He was one of the few people around here who went to college. Gabriela got up and ran over to him, lying her head on his thigh. He patted her back to acknowledge her.

"So long as people weren't breaking down the government's doors demanding things, complaining, and all paid their electricity on time, no one bothered each other," Héctor said in a slow, melodic tone. He smelled like jasmine and juniper.

"I hear you. My first day at the center: seventeen kids. I put them in a row of chairs, dressed myself in plastic bags, and went down the line, picking lice out of their hair. Some showed up without underwear. No shoes! I clipped their toenails and fingernails. Some of you scrubbed their hands. You know not all of that was dirt," Mamá said. A righteous smile creased the corners of her eyes.

"Do you remember? The next day there were fewer. Some parents were so embarrassed that they had sent their child to day care and that we had cleaned them up that they didn't send them back," the woman from the *soda* said.

"Families living here can save a good deal of money. No rent, no water bill. So many just sit back waiting for someone to give them things in this life," Ricardo said, lifting his eyebrows after every sentence.

"Worse are the times when people *do* give them things. It reinforces how they live. People want everything for free," Mamá said.

A few people looked down, shifting in their chairs, growing uncomfortable.

"Parents who live in shacks have children, and their children have children, and they build another shack behind the first one and stay there forever and nothing changes! Some parents come to meetings just to ask *me* to feed their child!" Mamá's voice was incredulous and firm, building to a crescendo. She sounded mad at herself. Her anger was disguised by layers and layers of exhaustion. A part of Gabriela understood. *Mamá worked so hard. Up at 5:30 a.m., finishing at 9:00 p.m.*

"If you don't teach your children, you will lose them here," another added, looking guilty that Mamá was the angriest and trying to match her intensity. They had tired smiles, too, just like Mamá.

"We used to be eight people on this board and now we're five. I'm tired of the community not realizing what we do for them and the city comin' in and tellin' us that we have to leave when they've given us nothing," Ricardo said.

"There's still so much to do, though," said Héctor. "If this *desalojo* goes through, the two schools around here will have to close or relocate."

"Has anyone talked to them?" Ricardo said.

"I just want it to be over." Héctor let out a resigned sigh. "I hear some people not from here comin' around with fake papers saying they have property here, all just to get the subsidies. The whole thing is rigged." The room fell quiet. Mamá had her thinking face on.

"What about a protest?" Mamá said. "What if we stand up to them? We've been playing nice all this time. Don't you think it's time for action?"

Several heads nodded around the table. Gabriela's attention trailed off. She slipped under the table and sat at Héctor's feet. She went back to her beach, to where no one was tired, where the sandy grout met the cool blue water, where Mamá wasn't struggling, and no one talked of subsidies or the volatility of this place just waiting to go up in flames.

CHAPTER 22

MOONLIGHT

Pepe sat splayed on the threadbare sofa, the remote control resting in his thick hand. Olga wasn't sure why he had come around, with his body languid while Mom flitted around their makeshift living room, moving things that didn't need to be moved. Jose was the only one happy to see him, sitting at his feet only reaching his knee, waiting for a glance, a half-smile, anything to acknowledge his presence. *The little guy just didn't know.*

Mom didn't seem to know what to do with herself, finding anything to do but speak. With him, words brought nothing but trouble, and here he was now, sitting in their living room, available. Olga sat hip to hip with Ariel on a stained red futon, more impatient than her mother.

"So, Papa." Olga cracked a smile, nearly laughing at his inadequacy.

He grunted. Even a question was too much of an imposition.

"What have you been up to?" she said.

"Ah you know, working here and there."

"*Qué bueno* that you're working!" Mom said, too enthusiastic.

He didn't flinch.

"The girls are restarting school soon, and *sabes que,* they might need a few things."

"What are you saying?" Pepe said.

Mom hesitated, still hung up on his every word.

"It never makes it home, that's what she's saying," Olga said, not regretting it, not even for a second.

He looked at Olga as if he knew she wasn't finished.

"You lose it in your *fucking* bottle!" Olga had never used the f-word in front of her mother. It tumbled out of her mouth, somehow perfect for the visit.

Pepe's knobby cheekbones tensed. He let the remote tumble to the ground. He looked so ordinary as he stood up, anger swirling in an aura around him. Getting a rise in him was exhilarating for her. He didn't deserve to live without demons, the ones he sicced on them more than she wanted to remember. He seemed to be calculating his next move, a terrorist suspended in time.

Pepe let out a small, sideways laugh. "Is *this* what you've created?" he said in Mom's direction, motioning to Olga.

Pepe lurched at Mom, shoving his shoulder into the rolls of her belly and knocking her down. Ariel screamed, and in a single movement, scooped up Josue and dashed into their room. Olga yelled at him and he yelled back, not stopping to hear what she said. Mom scurried her legs against the floor that had tiles but no grout, scooting her butt backward as they tilted beneath her weight, aiming nowhere. Forgetting what was at stake for her, Olga jumped on his back as he hunched over. He smelled of cheap beer. Mom rolled to her side, barely able to get to her feet. She burrowed into another room, concealed for just a moment. Fear-sweat hung fragrant in the air.

Olga pulled at his face, but it was swollen, damp, and hard to grip. He swung her around, sending her tumbling over the futon and onto the floor. A raging pain crept up her wrist.

Pepe turned, leaving her there, pounding toward the room where Mom was. He lifted his leg and punched through the fiberboard. *He surely could have opened it normally.*

From where she lay, a semicircle of moonlight gleamed through their front door. The light vibrant and blue over their tattered welcome mat covered uneven packed dirt that felt their every step. It knew every story, every rant, every explosion of epic proportion, best fit for a sci-fi movie. She thought about running. Getting out. Going anywhere but here.

Pity lifted her to her feet as she pressed her hands against the futon, dense and decrepit. Her footsteps kept pace with the blows. As her face came into the frame of the disjointed threshold, she saw him lift his elbow once more, clutching Mom with one thumb on her clavicle and his bulky, tired hands suctioned to her shoulder. She saw that he felt her presence. He stopped and looked back at Olga, melting before her. He began to weep.

Olga had never seen her father cry.

Mom shuddered and slid off the bloodstains on the sheets. He didn't even seem to notice she was gone. After a few salving sobs that served only himself, Pepe looked up at her, expectant, waiting for instructions.

"Leave." Olga's voice was steady and enraged.

He lifted himself off the bed and looked down at the blood on his shirt, suddenly confused and afraid of himself. His bulky stature wobbled out of the room, stepping over the broken boards that laid bare what he couldn't contain. There was nothing left to say.

Olga slammed the plywood door to her room, anger and sadness fighting each other, neither winning. Prone on her worn quilt blanket. From the sideways view of her world, Olga saw two tearful faces peer through the crack in their off-kilter closet door.

"It's fine, come out. He's gone." The bed distorted her cheek, making her lips fishlike as she spoke.

Ariel nudged the door open and Josue crawled out, his eyelids stained and his brow furrowed. His little brain was clearly in overdrive trying to make sense of it all. Ariel seemed rebuffed, both somehow upset at what just happened and slighted that perhaps she didn't know more and couldn't indulge in her anger the way Olga could. *All the times Ariel didn't see. All the times Josue hadn't even been born.*

TV commercials played unperturbed in the other room, their vanities once entertaining, now taunting. Olga's analogue clock rusted around the edges read 11:18 p.m.

"You know what we have to do?" Olga remained doubled over on the edge of the bed, arms flopped at her side.

"Huh?" Ariel said from her cross-legged position on the floor.

"Go to court." Olga let out a guttural sigh that rippled through her whole abdomen. It lifted her off the bed like those inflatable tube men that danced around on the side of the highway by the gas station, red, aimless, yet tethered. She had forgotten about the pain in her wrist for a second, guarding it in her other hand as it swelled. She could still sort of move it.

"We also can't stay here. He's crazy," Olga said, propping open their plywood door. Her mother was draped over herself on the sofa, bruised, with blood bulging from her upper lip, fixated on the remote control on the floor. That was all he left in his place.

"Mom, drinking is one thing, but you can't let him hit you like that. A divorce isn't enough. You need a restraining order," Olga said.

Mom propped her chin on the heel of her hand.

"It's so extreme, the divorce was so . . . *ya sabes,* I just . . ."

Olga cut her off, raising her voice. "No child support in a year, and he thinks he can come around here and act like that. He could come back tonight. Don't think it's safe here."

"It's not safe out there either."

"Well, take your pick. And you need bandages."

Olga had already told her mother to file a complaint the last time this happened. Standing up for her again. Olga was sick of suggesting things. She tilted her head, motioning toward the cracked door. Modest and soothing, moonlight now flooded their shack. It knew exactly what to do.

Olga scuttled open the front door, and they all walked out with Josue was on her hip. She locked the door behind them as if he couldn't kick through that, too. Cicadas pattered in the trees above, disguising their every step with rhythmic clicks. Sores on her chin still stung. Olga kept her head on a swivel, waiting for him to see them. At once, she felt sick, reminded for a moment that a baby was coming and hoping, for the first time ever, that it was still there.

CHAPTER 23

THE VISIT

Armon lifted the metal horseshoe keeping the squeaky gate in place. Green vines twisted around the metal poles, subsuming the fence and pulling it down. He heard a woman's voice shouting from the house a block away. A few boys sat sprawled on the sidewalk against a wall. Armon's feet pounded the wet ground. He walked down the dirt steps, making sure not to look over the edge. He had always been afraid of heights.

Wearing his best shirt, Armon approached the shack. It had fresh dirt all around. The front was decorated with tomato plants, flowers, and half-cut tires. Face to face with the door, he inhaled, the pungent rot of dead foliage all around.

"Is Doña Xianne home?" Armon said to the door, raising his voice so they heard.

A woman came to the doorway dressed in loosely fitting jeans, sandals, and a spandex top showing the rolls in her belly.

"*Soy yo*," she said, lowering her voice. Xianne's skepticism hung in the air, defending the territory of her front yard. Beneath it, she had an arresting smile.

"I'm Armon. I know we haven't met before, but I work with the center." As the words tumbled out of his mouth, shame crept up his neck. It was higher-caliber deception.

She eased, and sadness blinked in her eyes for a moment. She closed the door behind her and stood in her yard. Her lip had a single stitch in it. Black and blue bruises traced the ridges of her shoulders.

"How can I help you?" she said.

Armon cleared his throat, touching his fist to his mouth. "I wanted to come around to check on how you're doing with the *desalojo*."

"These days have been *bien duros*." Her voice dropped an octave as if trying not to cry.

"I hear you."

"It's been hard to know what's real, who to follow. Jimena told us to get a subsidy. It's so complicated." Xianne paused, as if "complicated" were just the beginning.

Armon let the silence hang.

"My . . ." Xianne tried to speak. "My . . . ex-husband, um, he just won't leave us alone." A single tear streamed down the outside crease of her eye.

Why was she telling me this? A perfect stranger?

"Last week he came 'round. We had to leave that same night. My girls pushed me to file a complaint at the court. Slept on the benches, there, you know? In the plaza?"

Armon's mind darted to the dark figure at the wake. The one at his house that night. Here in front of him was exactly what he needed; some son of a bitch had just made it all very easy for him.

"I've slept on benches. I know what that's like," Armon said.

Xianne looked him straight in the eyes, brushing away her own tear.

"We just moved here a few weeks ago from across the *precario*. We were told we were too close to the water purification site up there in Sector 4."

"You know they're just trying to squeeze you out, one way or another. And those subsidies? Those can't be real. Just their way to get people to give up their land."

"Well, *gracias a Dios,* we'll find a way."

"You're from up north, right?" Armon said, referring to Nicaragua.

Xianne didn't answer. Her pudgy brow crinkled, depleted and apathetic.

"I have a way for you to get out," he said.

The muscles in her face lifted.

"I can get you anything you need. You need me to take care of that ex-husband of yours? Protection for the trip? I can make that happen. I could even get someone to pay for your land before you go," he said, sweetening the deal beyond what she could refuse. He sensed that she wanted to believe.

"What do you have in mind?"

"I have some bags that need to go north. If you're heading that way anyway, I'll drop them off before you go."

"Is it illegal? Because I can't have that," she said, averting her gaze. "My cousin was in for four weeks. He came back a different person."

Armon stayed silent. Part of him couldn't believe what he was asking her to do, while the other part knew he had no choice. It was either this or his life—just like Tolte.

"They even stole his shoes." She stopped and looked at her hands, picking at her nails. "I sell CDs down at Paseo Diputados every day and one of my daughters is pregnant. I can't get wrapped up in anything like that."

"It's not illegal, especially if you don't know." He diverted her attention away from what she stood to lose.

She exchanged a knowing glance. *Did she know this was all a trick?*

"*Sabes,* people like us will always be stuck in problems like this. It's only faith that will carry us through." Her voice was calm and measured. It seemed to surrender to form a deep courage and inner balance.

Armon was surprised by her sudden confidence, an affront to what he was trying to do.

"How far has faith gotten you?" Armon said.

"How far have the actions of men gotten *you*?" Xianne asked. Her emotional exterior hardened.

"Do you want out or not?" Armon said, as if it were his final offer.

"Whatever this is, I know it's not right, but neither is this *desalojo*, or what my kids had to see the other night."

"I'll take that as a yes," Armon said.

Xianne dropped her head, inhaled, and nodded in affirmation. She looked disgusted at him. *But what other option does she really have?* He was doing her a favor.

"Don't tell me more than I need to know. And what we'd really want is a place in Jinotega. Away from here. Where he can't find us."

"I'll see what I can do."

Armon headed back up the hill, weaving his way through the plastic orange road barricades. Nothing to do now but wait, alone with the thought that he had just let fear win.

CHAPTER 24

THE BRIDGE

———

Gabriela raced up and over makeshift porches, weaving between steady trees and rotting wooden pallets. Her shoulders brushed the tops of plastic barrels full of musty rainwater, splashing her as she went. Mamá had left the house so quickly. She hadn't even had a chance to lock the door. Gabriela had to go help Mamá with all the commotion. She had to be brave, just like Mamá taught her.

Just over the hand-built roofs, Gabriela could see an uneasy crowd. Heads bobbed as they marched toward the bridge at the bottom of the fire road. Gabriela bounded down the hill toward the scene, which grew more volatile with each step she took. Her little legs couldn't move fast enough.

As she approached, she heard people shouting, though she couldn't decipher it all. Her chest tightened.

"¡Cabrones! Git!" one person said above the din.

Glancing up for just a moment, she stopped to calculate her path through the crowd to reach the bridge.

Putting her hands together in front of her, she dove between the legs, wedging the tips of her fingers in between hips of all sizes. As she wove through the crowd, the weight of other bodies started to carry her. Her feet lifted off the ground.

She took in all the different colors of pants that people had and thought about staying where the colors were, but she thought Mamá must be at the front, and she couldn't let her go to it alone. She had to get to there.

Gabriela emerged to the right of the crowd on the shallower side of the embankment where the water had been rising ever since the earthmovers visited. Across the bridge on the Monte Verde side, Gabriela saw a few men standing erect in their charcoal gray uniforms holding their hands firmly behind their backs. Their guns were never too far away. White government vehicles dotted the other side of the bridge.

The trunk of her other favorite tree had a ring of bright green algae around it and the creek now covered its roots. It stood out from the brown water that carried wads of trash into eddies that would still be there tomorrow. Soggy T-shirts, plastic netting, and campaign posters swaddled the trunk. The tree was unmoving, not letting them pass by the spatchcock huts that teetered on the alluvium.

Gabriela recognized everyone. Many of her neighbors lined up facing the vehicles on the opposite side of the bridge where the *precario* started. Alejandro was there—he was her size—even Olga, Ariel, and Patricia had found their way to the front. Gabriela wanted to be with them.

She descended the embankment. Her galoshes suctioned to the silt. As she lifted her foot, the strap across her ankle broke. She tried to move quickly along the water's edge, scaling where the bridge met the ground. Gabriela pulled herself up and squeezed her way to the line of people crossing the bridge, sidling up to Patricia. All the adults stood resting their hands on their kids' shoulders. Even Ricardo, Héctor, and Layla were there: all the people from the meeting. The police and government people looked more intimidating up close. The crowd was insatiable.

"You're in the wrong neighborhood!"

"Our lives are here!"

"You give me one good reason to move!"

People bellowed at the resolute government officials. Gabriela recognized some of the words they were saying and twisted her fingers to make them out in sign language. She opened her mouth wide, mimicking them. In times like these, Gabriela wished for a voice, for something, anything to come out of her mouth.

"Last time this happened they ended up tiptoeing away. Couldn't take the heat!" a man yelled to the people around him, laughing.

A thin woman stood in front of the police in a striped long-sleeved shirt, her hair in a low ponytail. She was pretty with her fair skin and straight teeth. Two other men stood there in blue suits. *Isn't it too hot for that?*

The fancy people standing on the bridge were trying to speak, but the crowd drowned their faint voices. Gabriela was curious to hear what they had to say. Everyone seemed so upset.

Gabriela felt an arm wrap around her shoulders.

Mamá! Gabriela extended her arms around Jimena's leg, happy to see her.

"Gabi, you can't be here right now."

Why is Mamá so mad? Just trying to help. Gabriela's shoulders drooped she tried not to cry. *Mamá doesn't like it when I cry.*

"Honey, this is dangerous, and I don't want to lose you in the crowd. Please, go home. I promise I'll be there soon." Jimena seemed to regulate her voice as she crouched to Gabriela's level.

Voices in the crowd surged and a wave of people lurched toward the bridge. Jimena shot up, craning to see.

"Gabi, it's not safe, you have to go, please! Up the hill, now!" she said, swiveling her head back in Gabriela's direction.

Gabriela's was thrown by the suggestion. All this time, Mamá had been showing how to be brave. How to fight back with love. Gabriela got one chance to prove she's brave, too, and Mamá shut her down.

Gabriela crouched down into a ball on the sodden ground as the crowd gushed past her. Jimena couldn't stay, standing up and pushing her way to the front of the crowd.

The crackled voice of a megaphone started raining down upon them, firm and confident unlike most people in the crowd, except for Mamá.

"Protective services are here. If you don't take your children off this front line, we'll take them into custody, and you will be charged with negligence."

It sounded like Fernando's broken robot toy he let her play with sometimes. He had dropped it out the window off the side of the hill once, and it never sounded the same again. It was the only toy that used to work. *Mamá was just as mad then.*

Gabriela picked herself up and clambered back toward the embankment to get a better view, wanting to see where Mamá went. Neighbors swarmed over the bridge. Many grabbed the children, sullied and scared in the front row, pulling them back, all the while shouting at the officials. Others stood in front of their children while police pushed them back with their sticks. The officials just milled around behind the police line, talking into their walkie-talkies with the long antennas. The police grew ornerier by the second.

Everything teetered on the edge. It was anyone's guess which way it would go.

Other people rushed away from the clash, wailing, looking confused and afraid. Gabriela had lost sight of the police in the mix and the pretty lady with the light brown hair, but Mamá was easy to spot with her washed-out black-billed hat she loved and wore on days like this. It undoubtedly gave her superpowers.

Mamá was short but seemed to command attention from the crowd. She moved through the crowd and pointed her arms repeatedly in the direction of the terraced shacks. Gabriela was transfixed by the way everyone let her by and tilted toward her. They seemed to be looking for answers, dizzy with the conviction she displayed and the scene before them.

A breeze drifted by, brushing Gabriela's hair from her shoulders. It carried with it the unmissable scent of burning tires—a persistent reminder that maybe they didn't deserve to breathe easy.

"By order of the district attorney, you have until Tuesday to vacate! And this time—" the voice paused. "We're not messin' around!"

The robot struck again. She imagined lasers coming from its eyes, beaming a violent red in all directions, indiscriminate and fierce. Gabriela felt safe up on the hill, watching her neighbors zigzag back through the slum lanes, corridors too narrow for any robot to venture.

Mamá emerged from the pack, solemn and head down. She had never looked so defeated. *Maybe bravery had a limit.* Behind her, the pretty girl had untangled herself from the crowd and walked back toward a white vehicle with a logo Gabriela couldn't quite make out, her ponytail not so perfect anymore.

PART V

PHEROMONE

CHAPTER 25

THE CLINIC

Olga peered up at the different signs hanging from the ceiling: Clorito Picado Clinic. Arrows were packed together in all directions as if they didn't even know which way to go. Mom and Ariel entered with Olga, their sandals clacking against the shiny, speckled vinyl floor with the low din of too many conversations in a small space. It had the aggressive smell of cleaning solution.

Mom hesitated and swallowed hard. Olga turned to her, wanting her mother to take the lead just this once. Mom looked at her sheepishly, clutching the cloth purse with a faux leather strap cutting across her chest. Ariel took her sister's arm, pulling herself toward Olga's shoulder.

Mom stepped forward, approaching the first desk. Many people waited in line. Olga and Ariel made their way to the light orange scooped-bottom chairs stuck together in a row. *When was the last time they were cleaned?*

Olga slumped in her chair, trying to readjust her waistline. Nothing seemed to fit. Ariel sat down for a second before rebounding and walking toward a plaque on the wall with an old photo. Olga rolled her eyes at Ariel's childish curiosity. Ariel stared intently at the wall with her hands on her hips. After a few moments, she came bouncing back.

"Clorito Picado! Do you know who he is?" Ariel said.

Olga was already bored with the question. She shrugged.

"A scientist. Full name was Clodomiro Picado Twilight. He discovered penicillin way before that British guy Fleming. And guess what?" Ariel paused only to take a breath. She seemed unbothered by Olga's lack of interest in this very empirical revelation.

"He wasn't Costa Rican. He was *nica!*" she said. "Nicaraguan!"

"I mean, Twilight's a pretty good name." Olga humored her sister. "Why didn't they name this place Twilight Clinic?"

Mom pivoted away from the attendant at the first desk and walked toward the girls with a spurt of newfound confidence.

"Okay, what we need is a copy of the electricity bill to prove we live in the *precario*," she said. "And a copy of your ID." She motioned toward Olga.

Olga nodded. "Gotcha. Let's go then."

"Thank God they didn't ask if we were *nica*," her mother added.

They got off the bus at Monte Verde where the city had just paved the road with smooth black asphalt.

The three turned down a corridor and walked closer together, knowing they were linked, if nothing else, to this baby.

They stopped at the makeshift convenience store and filed into the narrow passageway flanked by every type of junk food imaginable. It smelled of a mixture of soap, marshmallows, pretzels, and *pupusas*. They made their way to the photocopier in the back. Ariel grabbed Olga's ID out of her hand to make a copy. Olga smirked but let her do it, knowing her sister had something to prove.

Slapping the ID card down on the scratched glass, Ariel pushed all the buttons. They waited as the run-down machine flashed blue three times.

"Twenty *colones*," the cashier barked from the front of the store.

Olga paced back through the rack of potato chips and dug into her coin pouch. She pinched two coins between her index and forefingers, placing them on the counter. The cashier swiped them up and dropped them into a plastic box.

Mom and Ariel trailed behind her.

Olga thanked the cashier under her breath and walked out, papers in hand. The metal security bars clanged against the threshold as they left.

The *precario* was quiet in the early morning. Only the normal hum of the highway and the roosters were audible. Retracing their steps, Mom, Ariel, and Olga made their way back up the incline covered half in concrete and half dirt. They emerged onto the fire road, taking a few steps up to Jimena's house, and ducked under linens, socks, and T-shirts hanging to dry on the line.

Olga knocked on the door.

"*¿Sí?*" Jimena's voice sounded older, or maybe she just hadn't had her coffee.

"It's the Campos. We need a copy of the electricity bill for the clinic," Olga said, talking to the closed door.

A moment passed. Jimena cracked the door open.

"Come in, come in," she said, wrapping her nightgown around her waist.

Wooden pallets meant for forklifts covered the dirt floor. Jimena motioned for them to sit on the stained couch and armchair propped up against the wall with yellow foam protruding from its base. Jimena lowered the volume on the *bachata* blaring from the boom box speakers. Blue lights lined the inside of the speaker and flickered with the beat of the music.

Belén sat on the dirt floor in her pajamas, playing with a plastic phone and cord that was missing the dialer. The parakeet's cage was on the floor next to her. It nibbled at the girl's short, curly hair as she tried to make a call. She couldn't be bothered.

Jimena pulled a few papers from underneath a stack of old magazines and newspapers and ruffled through a basket of knickknacks on the table. Her hand emerged with a pen.

"Okay *mija,* spell your name please," Jimena said, situated herself in an overstuffed chair. Mom leaned forward before Olga could speak.

"O-L-G-A C-A-M-P-O-S," Mom said quickly. Jimena looked up, surprised.

"And where do you live?"

"Sector 1," Mom said.

"Who do you live with? Full names please."

"Mom. I got this," Olga said. Mom sat back in her chair. "Josue Campos, brother; Ariel Campos, sister; Xianne Campos Mirada, mother; and sometimes, Aunt Carmen Llora, and a cousin, Katia Llora." Olga paused, delaying the inevitable. The family barely fit onto the lines of form just like they barely fit in the same house. "And Pepe Campos, father." She could barely say the word. *Father.* It knocked the wind out of her.

Jimena squinted her eyes and interrupted. "Oh no! I made a mistake. I have to redo it," she said, setting aside the piece of paper and pulling out another from the stack. "Now, tell it to me again," Jimena said, staring down at the page intently.

Olga stared back. *Patience.*

She repeated all the names, but this time, left Pepe off.

Finishing the form, Jimena held it out across the room toward Olga as she stood up to take it.

~

Documents in hand, Mom approached the window at the clinic again. "I have the copy of the ID and the electricity bill now," she said, Olga by her side.

"Go to the back of the clinic and check in at the pregnancy ward," the woman said, pointing toward another desk with a sliding window. Mom nodded and walked toward the second window with a labyrinth of people extended from it.

An eternity passed. Olga stepped up to the window. The clerk collected the papers.

"I'll issue you an insurance card valid for one year of prenatal care," she said, handing Olga a slip of paper with the number forty-six on it. "You'll have another appointment scheduled for next week with a gynecologist."

Olga nodded in silence, pretending she knew what that meant.

"Head over to that waiting area over there and someone will call your number," The clerk said.

Many families sat around, fanning themselves with paper. Time slowed down. Olga didn't like being patient. She wished everything would move quicker. She'd change that, too, when she was elected.

A woman in a white gown and powder blue pants opened the door.

"Forty-six!" she said.

Olga perked up. She walked toward the nurse and looked back with genuine relief, catching her mother's eye for just a moment.

CHAPTER 26

ROBOTS

Bleeping noises pierced Gabriela's dream, popping it like a balloon. She awoke slowly, nestled among her handmade quilt that *abuela* had made her forever ago. Gabriela untucked herself from the blankets, bleary eyed, and wrestled her foot free from the sheet that wanted her to return to dreaming.

Gabriela found her way to the window cutout and pulled herself up to see. Bulldozers and metal dumpsters congregated on the Monte Verde side of the bridge. No one had moved houses and some people were standing in line at Layla's *soda* for breakfast, but the robot was getting ready anyway.

In her flannel onesie and pink Styrofoam Crocs a few sizes too big, Gabriela made her way to the first floor and walked out the front door onto the fire road. The fabric covering her feet was worn, so it flapped at her ankles as she walked down the hill. She carried her pink plastic plate with a thousand cuts on it, making the eating surface fluffy. She tiptoed around the broken glass, her feet slipping in her shoes.

A group of young men were gathered, leaning against a car near a makeshift kitchen by the bridge. One was skinny and tattooed and sat in the driver's seat with the door open, cleaning a switchblade. Next to them, some older locals sat together in a circle. One plucked a wire strung between a cardboard box and a pole like an upright base. Another struck his calloused hands against a wooden box, mismatched to the beat of the base. A few others lingered around humming, smiling, and bobbing their heads, unbothered by the off-kilter cadence.

No one in the neighborhood seemed to care about the impending robots, or maybe didn't haven't a single idea about how to stop them.

Gabriela approached the bottom of the hill by the bridge. Layla's wooden table was topped with two hotplate burners. A short line of people waited for food. Yesterday's rice mixed with slow-cooked red beans tossed delicious, oily aromas into the air. *Quesillo* fried in a pan. An extension cord draped down the side and slithered across the damp ground ending at an electrical outlet on the side of someone's hut. Frayed, scraggly wires bunched up on the sides of the outlet.

Gabriela bounded her way to the front of the line, extending her plate as high as she could.

"Gabi, you have to wait your turn," Layla said, serving a plantain with tongs to the first person in line.

No one else in line seemed to mind. Gabriela grunted and stretched her arm higher, trying to cover the top of one of Layla's pots.

"No, sweetheart, back of the line. It's short. Don't worry, plenty of food," Layla said.

Gabriela whined and thought about crying to get her way.

Layla went on serving other people, taking a few coins they scrounged from their tattered pockets and purses.

The bulldozer parked nearby turned itself on, catching Gabriela's attention. It let out a cloud of gray soot from the exhaust pipe, casting a temporary shadow over her.

All the neighbors in line turned in autonomic reaction to the squealing and hissing of the machine. *The earthmover that scared Mamá—there he was. He must have a heart. He'd know better than to destroy thousands of lives here.*

The earthmover rotated its snout. The wheels started turning in Gabriela's direction. It lumbered up to the narrow concrete bridge and started to cross.

Gabriela hadn't gotten her food, but this looked serious. With her plate in hand, she ran around the line and toward the bridge to get closer. No one else moved. The pads of her onesie flapped more aggressively against the tops of her feet as she maneuvered. The bunny ears on the head of her onesie bounced around.

Gabriela made guttural sounds, lifting her arms to the sky as she ran toward the earthmover. It was gunmetal gray. She looked it straight in its glass window eyes, but the bull-dozer just kept coming.

"Gabi, get back here!" Mamá yelled. No one else reacted. *Did they know something she didn't? Mamá had a way of always showing up, always being there.*

Innocence on full display, Gabriela turned to see her mother and the other onlookers. Gabriela used every sound she knew how to make, raging against the robot.

"Gabi, please!" her mother called out again. The bulldozer wouldn't let up.

"Gabi! No!"

The robot had crossed the bridge, and other robots were following.

She dropped her arms and the plate to her sides. The bunny ears fell quietly to her back. Even they knew.

Her head drooped, too, as if to bow to her mother, who was bowing to the earthmover, who was bowing to the pretty minister, the people in suits. *And who were they bowing to?*

Jimena enveloped Gabriela in her arms as the bulldozer carried on. Gabriela started to cry, real tears this time. She was sad for Mamá. She was sad for her neighbors, and her favorite *soda* that sometimes let her cut the line. She was sad for her friends, for the center, for her favorite tree by the creek. But mostly, she was sad for the earthmover, missing out on a chance to know them, realizing what they had in common, and seeing how they could work it out.

Jimena nuzzled her head in Gabriela's neck. *Was Mamá crying, too?*

The bulldozer struck its first blow, going after the shacks closest to the creek. The crash rung out through the whole *precario.*

"It's done. Let's go, *mi amor*," Mamá whispered.

The crunching and cracking of sheet metal, plywood, furniture, and satellite dishes penetrated the morning. Everything was happening in slow motion. Wooden beams, TV screens, mattresses, dishes, posters, blankets, pillows, silverware, electrical wires, pots, and pans came crashing down in an instant. It all collected in a heap of rubble, pushed around by the bulldozer's blade.

Perhaps the earthmover sitting on his perch didn't see it that way; maybe it was just the job he was assigned today. Never mind what Mamá fought for. What was right or wrong, who was brave and who wasn't. The fact remained: it was gone.

Gabriela stood tucked under Mamá's arm as they turned to walk up the hill.

CHAPTER 27

FOLLOWERS

———

Olga reemerged from behind the heavy metal door of the doctor's office, motioning with her head to her mother and Ariel that they could leave. She held a stack of crinkled papers in her hand.

"I'm fine. Just a small infection. Easy to fix. They gave me some cream," Olga said. "Oh! And I'm just a few weeks away!"

"Wow, *mija,* I'm so proud of you," Mom said, as if she were about to cry. That might've been the first time she'd said that to Olga.

"It's no big deal, Mom," Olga said, giving her mother a big hug.

Holding their embrace for just a moment, they made their way out of the clinic and headed down the street.

"Someone from that clinic was in the *precario* last week, knocking on all the doors. It woke me up! The guy said he was looking for someone who'd recently been seen for meningitis," Ariel said. "What's meningitis?"

"It makes your brain swell," Olga said.

"Ew, gross!" Ariel said.

"They shouldn't-a been goin' door to door anyway. Exposing people's information like that," Olga said.

As Olga and Ariel batted back and forth, Mom looked over her shoulder.

"Mom, what's up? You seem anxious. *Tranquilo.* Relax," Olga said.

"It's nothing, everything's fine. We just need to walk a little faster," Mom said, wrapping her arm around the air behind her daughters.

This was the fastest her mother had ever walked.

Mom's eyes darted about.

As they approached one of the *sodas*, Mom pointed to a narrow passageway.

"Mom, this is crazy. Why are we taking this way home?" Ariel said.

"Please, don't ask questions, *mi amor.* Just do as I say," Mom said.

They squeezed through, turning their bodies sideways so they could fit. Olga's stomach scraped the concrete wall. They turned the corner and inched their way between the back of the building and the fence. They broke out into an empty lot full of weeds.

"Ariel, I know you can climb. Please head for that fence and meet us at home. I'll go with Olga the long way around."

In rare fashion, Ariel rolled her eyes.

"This is nuts! What's gotten into you?" Ariel said. Obeying, she took off jogging toward the fence.

"Go! Faster!" Mom called out to Ariel. She scaled the fence, sticking her tattered sneakers into each hole. Ariel eased her way up and over the other side.

"Are we being followed?" Olga said. "Is it Pepe? Does he know?"

"I can't say," Mom said.

Olga hated being on the outside of anything that seemed adult. They crouched down in the lot for a few moments. The weeds fluttered in the wind, leaving Olga with an uneasy sense of quiet.

"Let's go this way, for a taxi." Mom stood up, crossing the lot toward another slim corridor. Mom didn't have money to spare on a taxi. They emerged on a street corner Olga didn't recognize. A line of pirate taxis idled.

"Are you free?" Mom asked. *A pointless question for a line of taxies.*

A guy with a t-shirt that didn't quite cover his belly was leaning against his unmarked car and fiddling with a toothpick in his mouth.

"Get in," he said, pained to have customers.

"Look, I don't have much. Can you just drive us around the block? I can give you ten."

Uninterested, he put the car in gear. Olga settled into the taxi with frayed upholstery and no seat belts. Something wasn't right. Mom wouldn't even look at her.

CHAPTER 28

BAGS

Startled by a loud crash, Armon ran out of his shack. The bulldozer was gnawing at the edges, scraping the entrails of people's homes, revealing the most intimate of details of life. There were three machines now and the police had shown up. No suits today.

"Shit!" Armon said under his breath.

He had to get out. Quick. This place would be teeming with police and his house was a goner anyway. Easier to leave amid the chaos. Armon hurried back inside and threw on a shirt and jeans, the ones from yesterday, hopping on one foot to get his shoe on. He threw a half-empty water bottle, his money clip, fake ID, one change of clothes, and a pack of candy into his Jansport, slinging it over one shoulder. Armon picked up two hefty duffle bags by the handles, wishing he didn't have to do it this way.

Armon kicked his own door open with his foot, his biceps flexing as he lifted the bags at his sides. He looked both ways and went for it, dashing through the slum lane for the last time. He breathed heavily, ascending the hill, slipping every few steps on the soggy ground, being sure not to make eye contact with anyone in case it still mattered at this point.

Armon emerged at the highway's edge, motioning to the first pirate taxi he saw. Just looking to make a buck, they never asked questions. Armon opened the trunk. In one motion, he slung the bags into the car. The creaky suspension bounced under the weight of them. Slamming the trunk closed, he ducked into the front seat.

"To the other side, top of the hill," Armon said to the driver.

"*Dale*," the driver said. "You in a hurry?"

"Yeah, demolition started on the south side by the creek. You'll probably have a lotta business today. Lots of people haven't cleared out yet."

The driver tensed his chin, making a frown of approval with his lips as he nodded. There was something in this for everyone.

The driver was on the wrong side of the highway to go the quick way. He dropped his foot to the floor, speeding down the highway, weaving between cars. Taking the next exit, he veered to the right onto a commercial street, hitting every stale yellow light that he could. Reds caught up to him, too.

Armon wondered if she'd still be there. News traveled fast through the *precario*. He couldn't miss his chance to move the stock. This was it.

Pulling up to the north side, Armon tossed the driver a few bills. *Probably more than it cost.* He got out and stood by the trunk. The driver wasn't opening it. Sweat squeezed out of Armon's pores. *What was this* chavalo *doing?*

"Hey!" Armon said. The car was still running.

"Hey!" he yelled again. Armon was suddenly mad at himself for putting them in the trunk. He just didn't think.

"Open up!" Armon said, slamming his fist on the rear of the car.

The trunk popped open. His heart lifted out of his stomach as he grabbed the bags and ran toward the gate.

Buried beneath the vines he saw a padlock. He dropped both bags to the ground, bending over to pick one up from the bottom. He heaved it over the fence, and it landed in a cloud of dust. Bending over again, he propelled the other up and over, even farther. His pudgy fingers clutched the flimsy fence as he curled his legs onto on the ivy-stitched barrier.

As he reached the top, a tear in his jeans caught the rusty edge, cutting his leg and tipping him off balance. He fell to the ground landing on top of his Jansport. One of the bags cushioned his head.

He got himself to standing and picked up the bags. He considered jumping down the embankment to avoid the stairs.

No, slow down. Armon exhaled and made his way down the stairs. It was a miracle they were still there after all the rain.

The door to the shack opened and Xianne came out, closing the door behind her. She looked relieved to see him.

"I was getting worried," she said as he approached.

"I'm here, I'm here," Armon said, setting the bags down. "Where do you want these?"

"Just put them on the side for now. The girls can't know."

"You doin' all right?" Armon said, putting his hands on his hips, trying to catch his breath.

"I heard it's starting, down by the creek."

"Yeah, was there this morning. It doesn't look good."

"We're leaving soon, I think. Waiting to see how far they come up today."

"Good."

"I don't wanna know what's in those, but I should tell you that we were followed last week."

"What? By who?

"Don't know. It was a few guys. I didn't get a good look."

"How far?"

"From the clinic to behind the *Pollo Rico* and we lost them there. I tell you, I was scared. Had to lie to my girls. You know I'm not about that."

Armon started calculating. *Who could it have been? They all want the drugs moved, what do they care how it happens?*

"I wouldn't worry. I'm running the traps."

A faint voice from inside their hut let out a shriek. "Maaaaa!"

"*¿Qué?*" Xianne said, turning her head in the direction of the shriek.

"*¡Venga!* Come here!" the juvenile voice replied. A girl's head pushed the curtain aside with a bandaged arm and peeked out, waving her other hand, signaling for Xianne to come. She didn't look at Armon.

Through the plexiglass, the brown-haired girl mouthed, "It's time! Water broke!"

CHAPTER 29

BAGGAGE

———

In Olga's arms was a tiny new life. Crusty skin, squinty eyes, and wispy hair. His body was so fragile. Tiredness overcame her. She released her head back onto the lumpy pillow; the florescent light encaged in dusty metal flickered overhead. She closed her eyes, holding Pablo close for one silent moment. She was a *mom* now.

Mom pulled back the curtain surrounding her birthing area, revealing rows of other shrouded beds. The screaming, cooing, and wretched sounds of birth cascaded on top of one another, making it impossible to tell what was mother and what was child. It smelled like latex and blood. Olga longed for fresh air. Mom's feet in socks and flimsy sandals shuffled against the clinic floor.

"*¿Cómo estás?* How are you?" Mom said, reaching over to take the baby from Olga's arms.

She bounced him against the crook of her elbow. His puffy legs found their way out of the swaddle. Pablo was unable to hold his head up against his grandmother's jolts.

"You know who's gonna to take care of you? You know who's gonna take care of you? You know who?" Mom's voice went up an octave each time. "It's me! You're mine," Mom said, nuzzling her face in his, singing a melody off-key.

Although exhausted, Olga still had enough energy to roll her eyes. Her mother was only kidding, but Pablo wasn't Mom's. *He was hers.*

Pablo started to cry, a beet red color flushed through his face and ears. He had the tiniest little cry, as if he were trying so hard to be obnoxious but just didn't have an annoying bone in his body. Olga closed her eyes and waited to see what would happen.

"I raised you and my sisters, and now I'll raise Pablo," Mom said. "He's hungry, Ol." She motioned for her to breast-feed. "That's a mother's responsibility."

"You like being a mother so badly, why don't you just do it?" Olga said, still with her eyes sealed, trying not to laugh.

Olga opened her eyes. Mom tilted her head and let her eyes rest at the top of her lids. Olga smiled.

Her mock resistance gave way to delight as she took Pablo back in her arms. He stopped whining and molded himself against Olga's skin. He was warm and suddenly content. Babies can be inconsolable one moment and so happy the next. A mother has that power. But Pablo must still like Mom *better.* Olga doubted herself for a moment as he began to suckle.

"He's a citizen, *sabes?* And you can be one easier now, too," Mom said, fiddling with the medical equipment beside Olga's bed.

"Yeah, but we have to go up north to get my birth certificate printed because *somebody* didn't bother to get one for me in the first place," Olga said.

"*¡Ya sé!* I know! There was just a lot to handle when we left," she paused, "We'll be back there soon; leaving Friday, actually."

"Friday? But that's just next week. Seriously?"

"Yeah, I don't want to wait around to see what happens with the demolition."

"But . . ."

Olga's looked down at her body, amazed it made it through labor. It looked more like Mom's now, still round like before. Her butt felt flat from lying there for hours and now it had to move.

"*Mira,* look, the bus is like 8,000 *colones* per person, so we can't go that way. We'll take it day by day, okay? Don't pack too much."

Olga was already drained at the thought: Walking out of town, then hitchhiking, then the back of flatbed, and sleeping in whatever little town they could find with people who didn't hate people like them—maybe catching the empty car of a north-bound train for as long as it stayed the center route. Dismounting to walk across the border to Nicaragua, find some bushes, scrounging for enough to share a taxi or local bus on the other side where it was much cheaper, and just hoping for the best.

All with Pablo.

And the smallest bag she could possibly pack.

Olga tucked rags into her shirt to help with the chafing. Her body was working in new ways just four days after giving birth. Three of her toddler cousins played like monkeys behind her. One ran out of the bedroom and returned from the kitchen with a metal pot, placing it on the ground, mounting it. The little girl grew about ten centimeters.

"I'm the queen! I'm the queen!" she said.

Another little one wandered in and peered into the bassinet where Pablo was sleeping. The third cousin was perfectly silent. His eyes were wide, observant, and perpetually stuck in time.

Mom was washing some Tupperware at the sink in the living room to pack food to take with them, flies touching down around her until she swatted them away.

"Ugh, I hate those flies!" Mom said, talking to herself. "Can you turn the TV down? It's so loud!"

They had turned their house upside down to pack, scoping out only their most precious things. All the rest would be swept away by the bulldozers that got closer by the hour. Four straight days of demolition. At least they didn't do it at night. Kids were running around everywhere with excitement. For what? They didn't know. They just loved the activity.

Olga pulled clothes from the closet and dumped them on the bed. She grabbed another armful of half-hung clothes, revealing two black duffle bags.

Olga knelt down, touching the rough edge of one, glancing over her shoulder for any little bystanders. They screeched and giggled in the other room. She pulled the zipper of one. Duct tape beneath. A hard surface. She peeled back the edges of the bag further, dozens of duct tape blocks stacked carefully one atop the other in rows and columns.

Drugs.

Pounds upon pounds of them. Olga closed the zipper with one swipe, leaning back from where she knelt, pausing at the altar of their closet.

"Ma?" she said, not raising her voice.

"Ma?" she said a little louder.

"¿Sí?" Mom appeared in the doorway that was still split at the seam.

"Should we take those bags in the closet?" Olga asked, in perfect teenage pitch, with almost perfect innocence.

The color faded from her mother's face for a moment.

Were they now in this lie together? Shrouded beneath the same condition of motherhood that demands sacrifice and shielding—a maternal martyrdom that arrived unannounced with that sweet little cry? The result of a perfect act of creation that bound them to the reality of their lives.

Mom didn't seem bothered by the question. Dizzy at the thought, Olga waited for her mother to lead the way.

"No, *mi amor*, no need. Just leave them. Too heavy and not enough room."

Mom looked down and dusted her hands against her thighs, tightly wound in her jeans. She exhaled all she could. Mom smiled. Olga didn't know what it all meant, but something stirred inside her—the gravity of a motherly decision taken and the thought of just how many of those she'd have to make from now on.

Mom turned to go back to her washing, grabbing the damp dish towel she had tossed over her shoulder.

Olga stood stoic in the doorway, left with the aching uncertainty that they might never be coming back, even if they wanted to.

CHAPTER 30

BASSINET

Armon tucked a handgun into the waistband of his jeans. The cool metal rested against his tailbone, held up only by his worn leather belt. He paced up the hill toward Xianne's house. Shacks in the *precario* were burning; some in defiance, others because power lines were down. The smell of synthetics ascended from the tips of the tongues.

The gate was open. He skated through, retracing his steps from before. This part of the neighborhood was quiet. No dogs barking, no music, no movement.

Armon approached the house, unsure whether to knock. *Would I give Xianne away?* Armon peered in the plexiglass window, seeing no one. He wrapped his knuckles against the door a few times.

No answer.

Armon noticed the chain wasn't tethered around the threshold. Unlocked. He pushed the door open.

"¿*Hola?* Anyone home?"

A cockroach crossed his path as he stepped over piles of clothes, overturned kitchenware, and furniture that had been pushed around. The metal pipe faucet was still dripping.

"Hello?" He called out again. The house was empty.

Good. They were on their way.

Armon poked around to see if Xianne had left him a sign, a place to send the money, anything. He walked into the first bedroom. It had an empty bassinet, tattered around the edges with a paisley fabric. He turned his head, staring into a closet.

The bags.

His mind calculated, putting the pieces together one by one. She just left them. Didn't even tell him. *Didn't she know what this could do to him?* He felt like running. All the fear and exhaustion caught up to him at once. *When you run from dogs, they always catch up.* It was better for him to stand his ground.

Pablo Coelho echoed though his mind: *You drown not by falling into a river, but by staying submerged in it.*

The bags.

He was still here after seventeen years. It was longer than he thought he'd make it. From a young age, the brotherhood loved him. They took him in off the streets and showed him the way. It was the only family he knew—but they also got him into this shit. Ordinary people seemed afraid of him whenever he walked around. Where did their fear come from? Had he acted that badly to serve their scorns? He knew he couldn't leave the gang. He was bound by the morgue rule. He was born to work for the gang. But what if he left? He'd be called a traitor. Armon couldn't get his head straight.

But the bags.

Do I want this life? Do I want to be running drugs, killing, stealing? Do I belong to this past? His nightmares no longer came with a cold sweat like they used to, just a faint feeling that he was choosing to stay submerged. Armon stood there and stared at the duffle bags. Did she ever even look inside?

There was something in him that needed to be free. He wished he could sleep deeper. He wanted to understand why these images stayed in his head. No one understood him. There was no one he could talk to. The spider web on his arm was a constant reminder that he was stuck forever.

This time, Armon would let them come to him. Xianne had been followed. They knew where to find him.

He paced around the room, glancing every few minutes toward the bassinet. *Xianne was too old to have a baby. Why was it there?* It taunted him. He never had that kind of love. All his life, he knew he was on borrowed time.

For the first time ever, Armon wished he owned a watch. The minutes stretched like Dalí's clocks—an artist he'd read about once—until he heard their voices in the distance. He couldn't make out what they were saying, just that they were approaching fast. For the first time since childhood, Armon was afraid. He wanted life beyond the gang. It had taken him this long to figure it out, but now he was sure. He'd meet someone. Build a family. Maybe even buy a home, or really find God. He'd choose differently from now on. *I promise.*

They didn't knock, kicking in the door to the shack instead.

"Hey! I know you're in here," one yelled. Armon knew they had guns drawn. He could feel it.

"In here," Armon said. The barrel of a .38 rounded the corner. Armon's arms resting by his side.

"Someone didn't follow directions," the voice said.

There he stood, face to face with *tercera palabra*—the highest rank in the gang. The tattooed face slowly worked all the saliva he had into the back of his throat with a sucking noise and released it with all the force his mouth could muster. Saliva stuck to Armon's face. He didn't bother to wipe it off, just waiting for what would come next.

CHAPTER 31

BE

———

Cristina fiddled with her prepaid cell phone, flipping it open and closed with her thumb nail. She sat in their living room atop several square, woven plastic bags of all different colors, listening to the bulldozers a few blocks away. Ma was running around the house, half keeping up with Jacob, who was now crawling, and half trying to decide which parts of their lives to bring and what to leave.

Maybe it was a good thing, all this. A chance to be jolted out of the normal, which was mundane to begin with. What new life might they create out there? At least it was novel.

Her phone rang and stopped as she closed it on accident.

"Shoot," Cristina said under her breath. Roger nudged her leg, looking sad and confused at all the commotion.

Missed call from Olga. Cristina called her back, holding the phone to her ear. It rang four times and a voice picked up.

"*Chavala*, I'm out front."

Cristina smiled and walked to the door, opening into their covered porch area, and out into the light.

Olga stood there with her torso wrapped in fabric. An extra bump around her chest.

"The baby! What is it?"

"A boy, Pablo," Olga said. Her flushed cheeks grazed the top of his head, which was barely poking out of the swaddle. Fuzzy hair topped him off.

Cristina ran to her, giving Olga and Pablo a big hug, stretching her arms as far around as they'd go.

"How was it? Giving birth and all?" Cristina said.

"Long and tiring, but he's here now," Olga said. "What's happening with you?" She motioned to Cristina's house.

"We're headed to Vaqueros, that land way out there. Ma figured out the subsidy thing finally. You?"

"North to Nicaragua." The whites of Olga's eyes turned red.

"I just can't believe it."

"How have things been with . . . you know," Olga said, touching Cristina's wrist.

"I'm actually talking to someone. A girl at the center helped me get sorted. And for free."

"Like a therapist?"

"*Sí*, a psychologist. She works down at the university. Sessions every week."

"Wow, that's great," Olga said, pausing, "Tina, I'll miss you."

"I'll miss you, too, *nena*." Cristina gave Olga another giant hug. Pablo started to fuss.

"Look, it might be a while before we can be in touch. We've got some things to take care of. Mom's in a bind, so if you can't find me, just know I'll try to be back one day."

Cristina was confused. "But wait, why?"

"I can't say. I have to go. *Te quiro*." This time Olga reached out and hugged Cristina, taking care not to crush the little guy. Olga let go and turned to walk away.

Cristina didn't know what it all meant. She just wanted everything to be okay. She watched Olga continue down the path until she disappeared around the corner. For the first time in a long time, Cristina was oddly content to be feeling something—anything—even if sadness. It was a glimmer of something real, a feeling she didn't have the urge to numb or to push down: just one to sit with until it passed on to something new.

CHAPTER 32

CICADAS

The men left Armon lying motionless, bleeding from every orifice, just as when he had been initiated late last year. This time, there was no one to take him home. This time, he couldn't afford to stay in bed for weeks. He rolled to his side. A shooting pain from his ribs.

The bags were gone.

He fucked up but was one of the lucky ones. They had pardoned him.

But why?

He had to leave, too. Not for the *desalojo*, but to avoid the *sicarios*—hit men. This was the only way this pardon would work. It didn't need to be spoken. He just knew. They didn't want anyone to know it was possible to get out alive. Armon couldn't be living proof of their flexibility, vulnerability, or worse, humanity; and yet sometimes, this is what they showed. As much as everyone wanted to believe that the gang wasn't made up of human beings, they were, in fact, just that, with all their own wounds that repeated themselves onto other people they harmed. It was an endless cycle Armon had, in his own small way, broken.

Armon peeled himself off the loose parquet floor, grabbing onto thresholds and furniture to stay erect. He stumbled his way to the front door. The daytime flooded his inflamed retinas. As much as he ached, maybe, just maybe, he had stopped running from his problems, confronting them for good. He'd go north like the others, maybe even back to Guatemala to find his family.

As he walked toward the stairs that he doubted he could manage, he took a step and the ground beneath him caved. A colony of army ants poured out from underneath his shoe, racing up and over his ankles and up his leg. He hopped around, beating his ankle with his hands, sliding into the dirt to rub them off. Some bit him and others dissipated, confused, and suddenly aimless. Armon fell to the ground. They had tackled a big, useless target.

Armon lay there for a moment in the dirt, panting.

His mind drifted up into the midday sky. The cicadas hummed above. He had never noticed them like this before, with their meditative sounds all in unison. He had never seen one, but he knew they were special beings. Cyclical and cautious, coming out only when they knew it was safe, waiting years upon years to emerge from their shelter in the ground. Listening to them chirp, Armon soon fell into a deep, deep sleep, one he hadn't experienced in years—content for just a moment with the feeling he might have done the right thing.

AFTERWORD

———

In 2019 globally, there were nearly 80 million people who had been forcibly displaced.[3] Forty percent of them were children and 85 percent of them were hosted in developing countries.[4] Most settled in cities.[5]

Displaced people I've worked with have told me the fear, uncertainty, and anxiety is overwhelming, and if you haven't had to experience it, it's hard to really know what it feels like.

In my view, this is what often gets lost in the public discourse and policymaking: the very profound, very human feelings of instability and being overpowered by forces way beyond most people's control. Also lost is an understanding of the havoc that trauma can wreak long after a community is gone, even when people manage by their own actions to survive.

———

3   "Figures at a Glance," United Nations High Commissioner for Refugees (UNHCR), accessed February 15, 2021.

4   Ede Ijjasz-Vasquez, Soraya Goga, and Ellen Hamilton. "Refugees and Internally Displaced Persons in Cities—The 'Hidden' Side of Forced Displacement," *The World Bank* (blog), May 22, 2019, accessed February 15, 2021.

5   "Figures at a Glance."

It is an experience more people will undoubtedly have as armed conflict, climate change, and their consequences make it impossible to live in many areas currently inhabited by millions—consequences borne of decades of action and inaction with frustratingly diffuse perpetrators.[6]

While we can rightfully debate optimal solutions, the first requirement, I think, is empathy.

By the time I first walked through Triángulo de Solidaridad in August 2013, there had already been numerous attempts by the Costa Rican government to evict the residents. First settled in 2000, Triángulo was situated on a terraced, voluptuous plot of land used for motocross and belonged to the Ministry of Public Works and Transportation.[7] Thieves posing as landlords would charge people for plots in the area—land the "landlords" didn't own.[8] Some paid, others didn't, and six hundred families settled.[9]

In 2006, *Sala IV*, the Constitutional Chamber of the Supreme Court, voted to displace Triángulo, promising to find an alternative location for the community. The 2007 Census documented all families that would be displaced. From 2008 to 2009, the Ministry of Public Health and Ministry

---

6   Kanta Kumari Rigaud, Alex de Sherbinin, Bryan Jones, Jonas Bergmann, Viviane Clement, Kayly Ober, Jacob Schewe, Susana Adamo, Brent McCusker, Silke Heuser, and Amelia Midgley, *Groundswell: Preparing for Internal Climate Migration* (Washington, DC: The World Bank, 2018), 2.

7   Costa Rica Ministry of Housing and Human Settlements (MIVAH), "Report on the Updating of Precario Settlements in the Greater Metropolitan Area," February 2005, p. 114-116.

8   Author's interview notes with community members. December 2013. San José, Costa Rica.

9   "Report on the Updating of Precario Settlements and in the Greater Metropolitan Area," page 117.

of Housing and Human Settlements (MIVAH) studied the conditions under which families were living and planned out several resettlement options.[10]

In 2009, MIVAH's minister of governance, police, and public security reregistered all residents of Triángulo in a government database, noting that none had rights to the land they were living on. The vice minister of public security had created an action plan in 2010 to displace the residents of Triángulo. The Supreme Court publicly stated that 525 resident families would be relocated to make room for high-rise condominiums.[11]

By 2011, the plan had not materialized, yet the idea still appeared in the city regulation plan for the Municipality of Goicoechea, along with plans to construct a highway that would alleviate traffic in and out of the capital.[12] *Sala IV* granted an eighteen-month extension for the displacement process that same year. The National Company of Power and Electricity (CNFL) performed another census that found 765 undocumented immigrants living in Triángulo, almost all from Nicaragua.[13]

That same year, government officials met with the community for the first time regarding the displacement process, which came to be called *el desalojo*—the displacement. The encounter ended in a street fight and officials left

---

10   Jenny Liberoff, Cinthia Carpio, and Lizeth Venegas, Costa Rica Ministry of Housing and Human Settlements (MIVAH), "Proposal for an Intervention Model in Triángulo de Solidaridad," May 2011.

11   Ibid.

12   "North Beltway Forces the Expropriation of 30 Companies," *La Nación*, April 9, 2014.

13   "Proposal for an Intervention Model in Triángulo de Solidaridad."

immediately.[14] By 2014, the three thousand residents living in this *precario* had been hearing about the possibility of a displacement for ten out of fourteen years.[15,16]

In 2019, the government ultimately displaced the residents of Triángulo, razed it in phases, and began construction on the highway that, as of the time of publication of this book, is still underway.[17]

Although not displaced, Los Cuadros de Purral struggled with a different kind of marginalization. It began as a legal, low-income housing project by the Costa Rican government in 1991 through Executive Decree 20587-G.[18] Located an hour-long bus ride from the center of San José, one main road passed Los Cuadros and ran through neighborhoods dotted with *precarios* and other more established housing.

Starting in the late 1980s, unable to afford other housing, people constructed *precarios* one by one every few years. By 2014, Purral was encircled by eight *precarios* – *La Lucha, Cervil, Pasos Verdes del Este, Las 85, Colochos, Luchando por un Futuro, Las Amelias,* and a nameless new one. Three

---

14 Interview notes with community members. January 2014. San José, Costa Rica.

15 Alonso Mata Blano. "Poems and Troubles in the Decline of Precario Triángulo de Solidaridad," *La Nación,* June 1, 2014.

16 Alberto C. Barrantes. "Days Are Numbered for Precario to Make Way for Beltway," *La Nación,* January 14, 2014.

17 "The Eviction of Triángulo de Solidaridad Reached Its Conclusion Today," Costa Rica Ministry of Health, September 10, 2019.

18 Eloísa Ulibarri P., Carmen González A., Anayansy Valverde, Rodolfo Gutiérrez, Rosendo Pujol, and Jorge Solano, *Eleventh Report on the State of the Nation on Sustainable Human Development: Housing and Precario Settlements in the Greater Metropolitan Area (GAM), Final Report* (Costa Rica: Foundation for Housing Promotion (FUPROVI), 2005), pages 7-8.

of those preceded the development of the formal housing in the Purral neighborhood.[19]

By the government's own records, the number of people living in slums from 1991 to 2008 increased, yet the number of slums had fallen. In 2005, the city of San José had 182 *precarios* registered, and by 2009, that number had decreased to 147.[20] It was both a matter of how they counted them and indicative of policies that caused an increase in density and volatility.[21]

Costa Rican policies toward informal settlements and people living in conditions of poverty fluctuated over time. In 1954, the Costa Rican government created the National Housing and Urbanization Institute (INVU) to address the needs of the poorest families. In 1966, the legislature passed a law for the eradication of slums and defense of tenants intended to promote "urban renovation."[22]

This law defined a slum as "any area, predominantly residential, in which streets, lack of services, as well as constructions or structures are detrimental to the safety, health or morals of the community, because of overcrowding, faulty design, lack of light and ventilation, sanitation or combination of these factors." Other urban planning programs developed in 1968 turned on the same idea that "urban renovation" was the solution to preventing and eliminating

19 "Report on the Updating of Precario Settlements and in the Greater Metropolitan Area," pages 114-116.

20 *Eleventh Report on the State of the Nation on Sustainable Human Development*, page 53.

21 "Report on the Updating of Precario Settlements and in the Greater Metropolitan Area," page 58.

22 *Eleventh Report on the State of the Nation on Sustainable Human Development*, page 7.

slums, and "lack of services" or "faulty design" was the fault of the residents.[23]

Meanwhile, the number of people living in informal settlements grew.

Not until 1971, with the creation of the Institute for Mixed Social Support, did the government acknowledge that in order to address the issue, families living in extreme poverty needed housing alternatives and the financial and social services to realize them. MIVAH was founded in 1980 with an unfunded mandate.[24]

In the mid-1980s during the Monge administration, the federal government tried declaring a state of emergency regarding the lack of housing across all of Costa Rica, stimulated by pressure from civil society organizations that recognized the dire needs and lack of services. In 1984, the government drafted a National Housing Plan and allocated emergency funds to the project. Policies calling for slum eradication returned, but this time, they were coupled with a national Mortgage Loan Bank to support the process of financing new homes in 1986.[25]

Still, by 1990, the creation of new *precarios* had reached a new high, in large part because of the influx of migrants escaping horrendous violence in northern Central America and its economic consequences.[26]

---

23   Ibid.

24   "Report on the Updating of Precario Settlements and in the Greater Metropolitan Area," page 8.

25   "Historical Review," BAHNVI - Mortgage Loan Bank of Costa Rica, accessed February 23, 2021.

26   "Report on the Updating of Precario Settlements and in the Greater Metropolitan Area," page 31.

~

Triángulo and Los Cuadros were two very different communities in structure, size, social dynamic, and history, yet were part of the same challenging national and, I'd argue, global picture of poverty alleviation efforts.

Costa Rica is listed by the Organization of Economic Co-Operation and Development as an upper-middle-income country: one too wealthy by measures of GDP to be the frequent beneficiary of foreign assistance or other financing mechanisms for their own domestic development.[27] As of 2011, nearly 1 billion of the world's poorest citizens lived in middle-income countries, like Costa Rica, *not* in lower-income countries.[28]

This not only puts into perspective the challenges experienced by lower-income countries, but it also raises questions about how countries at the middle-income level can ultimately become more prosperous, equitable, and sustainable societies. If we agree more outside money isn't the answer, what else must change?

The temptation from the government's point of view, as in the story, is *not* to grapple with the harder dimensions of sustainable development. It is instead to squeeze out low-wealth or immigrant families using any means possible to "make way" for well-meaning, arguably legitimate projects benefiting the broader economy.

27   DAC List of ODA Flows, s.v. "Costa Rica," by Organisation for Economic Co-operation and Development (OECD), accessed February 15, 2021.

28   Andy Summers, "The New Bottom Billion: What If Most of the World's Poor Live in Middle-Income Countries?" *Center for Global Development,* March 18, 2011, accessed February 28, 2021.

But the question to ask is: Who wins and who loses in this scenario?

Overemphasis on the national-level picture of economic development or on housing as "just" an infrastructure problem can stratify people even further. Investments are made that push people who already live just a few feet apart, yet under wildly different conditions, even farther apart. This was the case between the *precario* and Monte Verde, with nothing but a bridge connecting them.

The streets and lanes of Los Cuadros and Triángulo physically did not exist on Google Maps in 2014 while comparatively wealthier neighborhoods were charted. It was yet another daily reminder that they weren't accepted. Closing the wealth gap is not just an economic question, but also a spatial and a social one, embedded in perceptions and realities spurring fear and keeping the classes apart.

In short, forced displacement isn't a development strategy, it's another manifestation of inequality.

Without an understanding of and plan to address inequality, societies, no matter the bigger economic picture, will not rise.

Costa Rica isn't alone in this challenge. Latin America is the second-most unequal region in the world after Southern Africa, and the wealth gap is steadily widening in places like the United States.[29,30]

29 Linnea Sandin, "Covid-19 Exposes Latin America's Inequality," *Center for Strategic International Studies (CSIS)*, April 6, 2020.

30 "Inequality Index: Where are the World's Most Unequal Countries?" *The Guardian* (blog), April 26, 2017, accessed February 15, 2021.

Among the more mainstream examples of global inequality laid bare, in 2014, Brazil hosted the *Fédération Internationale de Football Association* (FIFA) World Cup, where reports showed contrasting stories of the realities of life in the *favelas* and the brand-new stadiums being built for visiting soccer teams.[31]

For decades prior, the human rights and development community had been working to highlight the levels of poverty and violence in the *favelas*.[32] However, the moral outrage over inequality in Brazil wasn't enough to stem the pressure FIFA could exert. The forced evictions around Rio de Janiero and São Paolo ordered by the federal government in the run up to the World Cup continued, and protests leading up to the games were continually squashed with police brutality.[33]

Under arguments of job creation, the infrastructure expansion was financed in part by Brazilian taxpayers, FIFA, and private donors, though it was clear that the $3.2 billion investment, in practice, would benefit only a select few.[34]

Similarly, news about the 2016 Olympic Games in Brazil showed sailors training off the coast of Rio de Janiero complaining about the trash and sewage floating in the water. They remarked that the numerous *favelas* perched on hills close to the coast caused runoff that would impact the health of

31 Owen Gibson and Jonathan Watts, "World Cup: Rio Favelas Being 'Socially Cleansed' in Runup to Sporting Events," *The Guardian*, December 5, 2013.

32 Pedro Strozenberg, "Brazil: 'This Is a Moment of Fragility for Civil Society,'" *CIVICUS*, April 25, 2019.

33 "World Cup: Rio Favelas Being 'Socially Cleansed' in Runup to Sporting Events."

34 Tariq Panja. "Brazil World Cup Stadium Could Be Used for Prisoners, Judge Says," *Bloomberg News*, September 24, 2013.

world-renowned athletes and the long-term environmental well-being of the bay.[35]

Perhaps most astonishingly, one Brazilian judge suggested that the Manasus stadium, located in an area where no Division I or II soccer team existed yet and built for the World Cup, be converted into a prisoner processing center after the World Cup to release pressure on the already overcrowded penitentiary system.[36]

Also notorious was the Tower of David in Caracas, Venezuela, a forty-five-story building project left incomplete when Venezuela was hit with the 1992 banking crisis and its primary investor, David Brillembourg, died. Construction was left unfinished on the third-highest skyscraper in the country.[37] People without homes began ascending the stairs and moving into every nook and cranny, creating a vertical slum that became home to three thousand people; the same population as Triángulo. They rigged electrical wires and water pipes as high as the twenty-second floor to incrementally improve their quality of life.[38]

There, too, evictions ensued in 2014.

And in Los Angeles, California, where my interest in exploring these issues first took root, homelessness is also on the rise. Despite yeoman's work by shelters and civil society to house record numbers of people, more are unable to afford housing

---

35   Simon Romero and Christopher Clarey, "Note to Olympic Sailors: Don't Fall in Rio's Water," *The New York Times,* May 18, 2014.

36   "Brazil World Cup Stadium Could Be Used for Prisoners, Judge Says."

37   Camila Domonoske, "Fall of the Tower of David: Squatters Leave Venezuela's Vertical Slum," *National Public Radio (NPR) The Two Way,* July 23, 2014.

38   Ibid.

and related services.[39] In the United States, one of the wealthiest countries in the world, wealth and income gaps are rising.[40]

In addition to the mirage that macroeconomics progress can create, there's a political dimension to inequality, too.

In the Costa Rican context, as a white, educated, privileged American, I found myself privy to conversations in which political elites who facilitated investments from overseas into Central America complained about "the eyesore of shantytowns when looking from the top floors of high rises in Guayaquil, Quito, Lima, and Panama City," laughing as they said it. They didn't think for a second someone like me would find their viewpoints deeply problematic.

These were their own countries, but where was the responsibility?

To me, there was nothing big or impressive about their thinking or their construction projects. It was just the familiar story of negligence, personal interest, and lack of desire for the public good.

In the early days of Triángulo, the government resisted the installation of utilities infrastructure: water, electrical, and sewage pipes.[41] Perhaps they thought that to allow those

39   Anna Scott, "Homelessness in Los Angeles County Rises Sharply," *National Public Radio (NPR)*, June 12, 2020.

40   Juliana Menasce Horowitz, Ruth Igielnik, and Rakesh Kochhar, *Most Americans Say There Is Too Much Economic Inequality in the US, but Fewer Than Half Call It a Top Priority* (Washington, DC: Pew Research Center, 2020), 1.

41   Interview notes with community members. April 2014. San José, Costa Rica.

services, which are, in fact, human rights, meant the migrants were there to stay.

It would also have meant acknowledging that there was a human element to all of it. Government agencies couldn't allow utilities to be installed without having egg on their faces for the existence of the *precarios* in the first place, appearing politically incorrect and outwardly inhumane for "allowing" the conditions.

Few with power wanted socioeconomic inequality to be at the heart of the political agenda, so they said all the right things and did many of the wrong ones. The perception was if they acknowledged the lack of affordable housing and the widening income gap, they'd have to do something about it.

Doing something would mean, among many things, challenging the small group of mediocre but influential businesses then-engaged in the construction of low-income housing.[42,43] Opening this market would mean angering those few stakeholders who had friends in high places. These companies were over-commissioned and under-producing. Corruption left a pit costing lives and well-being.

Meanwhile, fake landlords all over San José were ready with open arms to sell land to desperate families that ended up with no rights to that land, and the cycle continued—illegal actions that gave the government a low-grade headache but never screamed for action.[44] Tackling rent-seeking behavior was certainly not top of their list and would benefit people

---

42 Alberto C. Barrantes. "INVU President Denounces 'Monopoly' in Social Welfare Housing," *La Nación,* June 3, 2014.

43 Aarón Sequeira, "Defender Resigns Two Months after Her Re-Election," *La Nación,* July 8, 2014.

44 "INVU President Denounces 'Monopoly' in Social Welfare Housing."

to whom they offered few opportunities to become citizens, and voters, anyway.

Allowing utilities to be installed would also mean recognizing they needed a sustainable immigration policy—no one's favorite topic. As a result, the resourcefulness and resilience that is the hallmark of locally led development became the government's nemesis.

Ultimately, demolition was the end, displacing not only lives but also the very problems they started with.

Inequality has been called a "wicked problem."[45] It's not that the Costa Rican government so badly wanted their motocross arena back, it was that decades of policies didn't address root causes, and in some cases worked against, not with, human survival instincts and became more entwined with new challenges.

So where to go from here?

I won't pretend to offer a comprehensive solution to this complex web in the final pages of this book—even if one existed—but I will offer a starting point, and that is:

If we invest anywhere or emphasize anything, it should be to build and maintain the policies, structures, and resourcing that enable people who have been historically marginalized to lead their own development—a potentially controversial, counterintuitive viewpoint when talking about informal settlements, immigration, and multigenerational poverty.

---

45 Ewart Keep and Ken Mayhew, "Inequality—'Wicked Problems,' Labor Market Outcomes and the Search for Silver bullets," *Oxford Review of Education* 40, no. 6 (2014): 764-781.

In my experience, when it comes to basics, people generally want the same things, for themselves and for their children, and, if given an opportunity, they will work to build the life they want. That life will, in turn, benefit many aspects of society beyond themselves. Research exploring the positive economic impact of refugees in host countries is providing evidence of a dynamic that has existed in practice for generations.[46]

It is time we fully acknowledge that the web of political, economic, social, financial, and environmental dynamics at play is currently affecting us all. By fostering belonging with the support structures tackling inequality and prejudice, people find their way, and the so-called Gordian knot loosens.

It is also time to question the mythology around rags to riches, a narrative that is the reality for so few yet is a tantalizing storyline. This narrative obfuscates the structural challenges people are up against that are not necessarily overcome in a single generation. People who accelerate out of poverty may do so through the help of effective institutional or organizational support and well thought out, just policies that put the people experiencing those challenges at the center of the approach.

Grit and luck—the two-legged stool of the elusive American Dream—will not solve our global, structural inequality, especially when resources have been so unfairly distributed in societies for so long.

What would it take to achieve policies and practices rooted in local leadership?

---

46   Michael Clemens, "The Real Economic Cost of Accepting Refugees," *Center for Global Development,* September 14, 2017.

It would take consistently building political will and curiosity for what closing the wealth gap looks like and how it could work. It would take championing the needs of the poorest citizens, starting with humanizing what they experience and seeing them as agents of their own lives rather than victims.

Political will would need to overflow and influence financial stakeholders to reckon with the impact extreme profit orientations have on marginalized people and the role they play in exacerbating inequality. It would take more than a few leaders to dare to reach across political divides in a meaningful way and generate a unifying message many could get behind. It would also take honest recognition of the experience of poverty, especially the resiliencies it creates, and a reframing of how we, as outsiders, talk about the experience in the first place.

There is a dominant narrative about the weakness, vulnerability, and at-risk nature of this existence that seems to ignore that the problem does not sit with the impoverished, but with the powerful. The experience of poverty is the outcome of a system that allows individuals to accrue unnecessary wealth, not give back in systemic ways, hold all the decision-making cards, take perhaps purposefully negligible actions for maximum marketability, and afford them the platform to convince many others to follow.

This negative narrative around poverty, focusing on what is lacking, has been created and rehearsed by people and institutions who have likely never experienced chronic deprivation themselves or have not taken the time to understand it.

What I saw over and over in these communities was not the "lack of," but the resourcefulness that such need created in residents, such as Jimena's fight for her community's rights. Demands on their abilities to fulfill their basic human needs strengthened them in many ways in spite of the intensity of those demands. As a result, many living in poverty exhibited a unique kind of intelligence that should continue to be supported in efforts to tip the balance of power in their favor.

They calculated risk differently from those that have never lived under such conditions and intuitively grasped habits of personal safety and security, which I had to practice consciously. People like Vivia and Xianne had a more rational organization of needs and interests than those who did not need to decide between basics.

Many managed money and other available resources in very creative, dignifying ways without anyone telling them to do so. They prioritized according to survival needs almost immediately when presented with choice. Food came before bus passes, clothes came before toys, and women drove decision-making even if they didn't control the pocketbook.

Many, like Cristina, had little to no tolerance for drugs, alcohol, and gambling, because they were surrounded by their abuse and the pain it caused. They were diligent, almost militant.

They quickly learned conflict resolution in daily life. It became a matter of life and death, as was the case for Armon, Damion, Toltero, and others. Being able to speak the "language of the street" was a critical skill to resolve issues that arose among peers. Actions and split-second decisions had to be measured and taken calmly.

Each day, they had to strike a balance between deterrence, self-defense, and maintenance of relationships with enemies and friends. They were constantly evaluating and acting on the balance of power between them and others. Managing their anger and fear, deploying empathy, and speaking directly and succinctly to potential attackers contributed to their survival. Much like Xianne and Olga, they knew how to work a system and get what they needed. As in Jimena's case, religious counsel and faith became their channels for overcoming resistance and constant disappointment.

Like all the children and teens in this book, residents had to ignore certain aspects of their surroundings and at the same time be aware of its deficiencies to be able to improve it. At some point, people needed to separate their self-worth from their surroundings and know the prejudices thrown at them were not measures of individual worth and capacity, but reflections of society struggling with its own pain and disappointment.

One of my favorite theorist practitioners, John Paul Lederach, when thinking about the impact of violence on communities like these, observes:

> The surprising insight from these lands is that survival requires the horizon of hope with indifference toward the impact of violence. Indifference does not mean that people don't care. Theirs is not the indifference of apathy. It is the indifference of the heroic but everyday journey. They do not allow repeated cycles of violence to kill their passion for life or derail their daily journey. They keep walking the terrain in spite of violence. This requires a selective indifference: The particular events that are out of my control will not restrict or destroy my life. When these events are repeated over and again, across decades and generations, it creates the pessimism of survival. The space where selective indifference and hope meet gives birth to an extraordinary irony: pessimism is a gift for survival.[47]

---

47 John Paul Lederach, *The Moral Imagination: The Art and Soul of Building Peace* (Oxford, UK: Oxford University Press, 2005), 55.

Above all, supporting local leadership and collectively climbing out of inequality requires understanding these social intricacies, and not looking at poverty as the problem, but at the parts of our society complicit in it and sometimes benefiting from it.

Beyond the social science and the economics of it, this change in our approach requires a level of humanization that must make its return to our politics at all levels—in Latin America, the region I've come to love, at home in the United States, and in the thousands of other communities worldwide.

Empathy dissolves fear. Community removes otherness.

ACKNOWLEDGMENTS

—

Some words of gratitude because books certainly aren't written alone.

I'd like to first acknowledge the consistent and reputable presence of Boy With A Ball Foundation Costa Rica (*Fundación El Niño y la Bola Costa Rica*) in the communities that this book is based on. With their model of empowerment and accompaniment, they served thousands of families each year. I'm grateful for the extensive volunteer program they had in place that enabled me to meet and build relationships with many residents. I'm indebted to the families that opened their doors to me for interviews, questions, and conversations, and especially to the young women and girls whom I spent the most time with.

I'm grateful to the former staff of Boy With A Ball Foundation who I had the privilege of working with. Their sense of humor, sense of service, and kindness were constant sources of inspiration. I'd especially like to thank José Francisco Aria Perez, Max Cabrera Alfaro, Raquel, Sergio, and their families. A special thanks to Emily Hedin for introducing us and for your own leadership in building community in Peru, Costa Rica, and Washington, DC.

Many thanks to Princeton in Latin America and the Chantal Paydar Foundation for the financial support between 2013 and 2014 to engage in this work, especially David Atkinson and Dr. Remo Moomiaie-Qajar. To my dear Nicaraguan host family, Dennis and Arturo Obregon, thanks for all the laughs between those self-inflicted six-day work weeks.

Starting the book process, I thought the hard part would be writing. I quickly learned that what stands between "liking to write" and being an author is the mountainous, treacherous path of publishing. For guiding me through, I'd like to thank all the staff and leadership at New Degree Press and the Creator Institute, especially my editors Clayton Bohle, Sarah Lobrot, Carol McKibben, and Jack Cohen. I'd also like to thank Brian Bies, Kristy Carter, Andrea Miller Hayes, Amanda Brown, Zoran Maksimovic, Gjorgji Pejkovski, Heather Gomez, Jess Nielsen Beach, Aleksandra Dabic, Hayley Newlin, and Lyn Solano.

What first hooked me into the idea of writing a book in the early days of COVID-19 lockdowns was the vision Eric Koester laid out for equitable access to publishing and the infectious energy he put behind it. Thank you for making this journey so fun and accessible.

I'm very grateful to all the early manuscript readers who provided feedback before the story knew where it was headed, especially Allegra Batista, Susan Blair, and Kate Reott for reviewing the entire manuscript, as well as Karen Erickson, Diana McDonald, Cat Sides, Peter Blair, Dr. Pamela Hines, Ashlee Thomas, Dr. Mary L. Doyle, and John C. Doyle, JD (retired) for key input that made this book better.

I'm grateful to my family, especially my parents, Mary and John Doyle, Eamon and Meghan Doyle, Susan Blair, Don Schlotterback, Patricia Doyle, and many other members of "the clump" for their constant love and support.

And to Peter Blair, for much more than I can write in a book's acknowledgments page—thank you for being my partner in all things, for supporting my career and creative pursuits, and for the full-throated, daily laughs that put all my troubles where they belong: in proper, Northern Irish perspective.

Finally, I'd like to thank the 150 people who bought this book when it was still in the concept phase and who served as an amazing community throughout the process:

Remo Moomiaie-Qajar, MD

Bernadette Nelson

Karen Stockel

Jeff Stockel

Mary Doyle, MD

John Doyle, JD (retired)

Priyanka Arya

Diana McDonald

Bobby "Mac" McDonald

Amy Clark

Rachel Carrig

David Cronin

Micaela Nerguizian

Honey Al Sayed

Russ Watts

Adam Hoy

Lissette Almanza

Tyler Mow

Noam Unger

Daniel Friedman

Allegra Batista

Maryellen Miraglilo

Marcellina Priadi

Bruce Thomas

Elizabeth Mendoza

Aron Vrieler

Daphne McCurdy

Glyn Noguchi

Kyle Beaulieu

Kathleen Smith, MD

Jennifer Marron

Lukas Hegele

Anakwa Dwamena

Tiffany Chen

Molly Teodo

Noelle Liao

Johanna Waltersson

Berit Ek

Adele Stewart

Philip Paulson

Anne Kenslea

Andrew Loomis, PhD

Joyce Duckles, PhD

Kim Persson

Neha Kumar

Jack Cheap

Stephanie Amoako

Sara Nitz Nolan

Julia Ito Landers

Kaitlin Fuelling

Andrew Kim

Igor Josipovic

Erica Barin

T. Chase Meacham

Joseph Cendagorta

Angelina Gonzalez

Lisa Schirch, Ph.D.

Matilda Hagerman, PhD

Katherine Sullivan

Carol Krause

Pamela Huntoon

Justin Millar

Kelsey Harris

Vanessa Kulick

Gail Morgado

Laura Fremont

Rebecca Wall

Liseth M. Robledo

Bruce Hemmer, PhD

Karen Atkins

Amanda Juliett

Molly Scott

Adam Thomas

Laura Mabie, MD

Kendall Cheap

Eli S. McCarthy, PhD

Caitlin St. Amour

Andrew Rennie

Peter Blair

James Cheap

Lydia Cardona

Kate Reott

Pamela Hines, MD

Meghan O'Toole

Shaun Rundle

Carolyn Aeby

Beth Goldberg

Anna Fogel

Burt Blanchard

Patrick Doust

Marilyn Diaz

Kristina Petrova

Erika Paulson, PhD

Justin Christopher Valassidis

Kathleen Samperi

Daphne Panayotatos

Alexandra Moran

Viviana Volta

Caitlin Conaty

Elmo Jansen

Catherine A. Wood

Steve Ross

Kathryn Chew

Patrick Giblin

Anne Peacock

Robert Dawson, JD

Johanna Dawson

Karen M. King

Ian Fang

Katryna Mahoney

Kaitlyn Pajerowski

Pam Schlotterbeck

Jaclyn Rose Markowitz

Emily Hedin

John Schlotterbeck

Marnissa Andreini

Anna D. Applebaum

Linn Haggqvist

Donald R. Schlotterbeck

Katharine Cheap

Erica Pincus

Katie Seckman

Emily Schlotterbeck

Sam Worthington

Vanya Erickson

Susan Blair

Roxanne Paisible

Julie Miller

Wendy A. & Ed Hirschman

Kate Wharton

Patricia Cheap

Anne Hunt

Frank Baquero

Karen Erickson

Allison Toufali

Eamon Doyle, PhD

Kat Cheap

Adam Fivenson

Eric Koester, JD

Cynthia Irmer, PhD

Deborah Willig

Kaitlin Carano

Jaime Belmont

Kevin Rachlin

Milly Beebee

Mica Bumpus

Conor Godfrey

Whitney Martin

MAIN CHARACTER LIST

———

Characters are listed by family unit, oldest to youngest:

Jimena (Mamá)
José
Gabriela
Fernando
Unnamed younger sister

Vivia (Ma) & Alonso (Papi)
Cristina
Patricia
Belén
Jacob
Roger the dog

Xianne (Mom) & Pepe (Pa)
Olga
Ariel
Josue

Armon

Neighbors
Ricardo
Layla
Héctor

GLOSSARY

Amor: love; in conversation, *"mi amor"* is a diminutive term of endearment.

Bajonazo: type of well-planned extortion in which an armed group observes the daily routine of an individual they want to extort and often get in touch with close friends or family of that person to extract information before intersecting their driving route or encountering them at their home. At gun point, they force the individual to go to an ATM to extract money or to their home where the group robs them.

Banco Hipotecario de la Vivienda/Mortgage Loan Bank: nationalized institution that provides housing subsidies to middle- to low-income residents to pay for housing

Barra: group of young men who are usually un- or underemployed and spend their time in the communities engaging in petty crime. Some also participate in local level drug sales.

Barrio: neighborhood, sometimes refers to a poorer neighborhood

Balazo: shoot-out or shooting, cross fire

Bien duro: used in conversation, it means "really challenging" or "so hard"

Burbuja: bubble

Caja Costarricense del Seguro Social/Costa Rican Department of Social Insurance: the national-level institution responsible for public health policies and services, including the public pension system

Cancha: soccer field or other sports field

Cansada: tired, exhausted

Cantón: spatial classification meaning "district"

Carapicha: derogatory term for someone that does not like to party

Carnada: group of drug runners, a direct translation is "bait" (see also: *corredor* and *mulero*)

Cédula: Costa Rican identity card that documents legal resident status, insurance coverage by the state, and access to state education

Chavalo/chavala: young man or woman, used in the general sense

Chequeos: adolescent girls and boys between the ages of ten and twenty years who seek admission into a gang by way of performing murders, extortion, and other crimes for the gang's benefit. *Chequeos* are expected to be available twenty-four hours a day, seven days a week to perform any act for the leaders of the *clika* to which they are seeking entry, and they perform most gang-related killings in Central America. They usually spend two years preparing to enter the gang and are expected to improve in their ability to successfully commit crimes without consequence from the authorities. Fellow gang members are observing their behavior for performances that show rectitude, loyalty, and a sense of identity that has melded with the gang. After completion of this period, *tercera palabra* will "invite" the *chequeo* to be initiated. If he or she survives the rite, the title of *chequeo* is dropped, as he/she becomes a homie or homeboy and usually receives his/her first tattoo (see also: *rito de iniciación*).

Chiquitos/chiquitas: term of endearment for a group of small children, usually kin

Clika/clica: subunit of a gang that can include hundreds of members that operates using a pyramidal power structure and chains of command. The hierarchy is organized according to the following titles, from least powerful to most powerful: *paro, chequeo, soldado/homie/homeboy/miembro, ranflero, segunda palabra, tercera palabra.* Above *tercera palabra* is the gang leadership.

Coche: car

Colones: Costa Rican currency, generally 500-600 colones is equivalent to one dollar.

Compañía Nacional de Fuerza y Luz (CNFL)/National Company of Power and Electricity: national-level institution responsible for the generation and distribution of electricity that serves approximately 37 percent of the population. It is a subsidiary of the national power company, ICE.

Convivencia: cohabitation or living together in close proximity

Corredor/corredora: male or female drug runner, or any individual porting drugs from one location to another (see also: *mulero/mulera*)

Corte: sudden power outage or a judicial court

Desalojo: literal meaning is displacement; refers to the eviction of a squatter settlement

Dirección de Migración y Extranjería/Department of Migration and Nationality: national-level institution that oversees and regulates the movement of people across borders coming to and from Costa Rica

Dueño/dueña: male or female head of a household or business owner

Equipos Básicos de Atención Integral en Salud/Basic Comprehensive Health Care Teams: system of basic health service provision overseen by the Caja Costarricense del Seguro Social that services clinics and hospitals at the municipal level

Frente Amplia/Broad Front: social-democrat, minority political party founded in 2004 in Costa Rica with a platform of democratic socialism, green politics, and humanism; colors are yellow and black

Guila/s: informal term for a young woman or man

Homie/homeboy: gang member (see also: *soldado*)

Instituto Costarricense de Electricidad (ICE)/Costa Rican Institute of Electricity: nationalized electricity and telecommunications company that oversees CNFL and Kölbi telecommunications

Instituto de Fomento y Asesoría Municipal/Municipal Development Institute: municipal-level institution that supports environmental protection, coordination among municipalities, and waste management

Instituto Mixto de Ayuda Social/Institute for Mixed Social Support: national-level institution for social promotion that provides services to the poor through loans and stimulus programs

Instituto Nacional de Viviena y Urbanismo (INVU)/ National Housing and Urbanization Institute: national institutional that supports territorial organization, facilitates solutions for housing, particularly for the middle class, and maintains a savings and loans system.

La Llorona: Hispanic-American folklore character who, according to some versions, killed or lost her child and goes on an endless—and eventually fruitless—search for her deceased son. The term can also refer to a woman who is particularly emotional and cries frequently.

Lucha: fight; refers metaphorically to the fight for daily survival in impoverished conditions

Mara: general term for a transnational gang; in Guatemala, *mara* can refer to any group of friends

Marabunta: colony or plague of ants; also means havoc

Ministerio de Obras Públicas y Transportes/Ministry of Public Works and Transportation: national institution that oversees all infrastructure policies, planning, and programs, including roads, waterways, and bridges.

Ministerio de Vivienda y Asentamientos Humanos (MIVAH)/Ministry of Housing and Human Settlements: national institution responsible for policies, planning, and programs in housing for all socioeconomic categories and holds the mandate to implement the Regional Plan for Urban Development in the greater metropolitan area of San José

Mulero/mulera: male or female drug runner, or any individual porting drugs from one location to another, refers to the word "mule" (see also: *corredor/corredora*)

Norteño/norteña: literally means northerner; refers to individual members of a loose conglomeration of gangs with connections to the prison system in Northern California; symbolism showing this association includes the letter "N," the number fourteen, the combination of four dots in a square and one in the middle; key rivals include sureños/sureñas that are loyal to gangs in Southern California.

Nube: cloud

Paliza: physical beating

Pandilla: street gang, generally smaller than a *mara*

Papeles: informal term to refer to the documents necessary to hold a legal residence in Costa Rica

Paros: young girls and boys usually between the ages of seven to fifteen years old who aspire to be *chequeos*. They choose to spend time with *chequeos* and other initiated gang members. They are not allowed to have tattoos, and for this reason, are often called on to liaise with local authorities in cases of emergency to ensure that the gang is not harmed (e.g., if a *chequeo* dies during the rite of initiation) and to assist in murders and extortion for the gang's benefit. Gang members attract *paros* (and *chequeos*) with material goods (e.g., leather jackets, food, etc.).

Partido Acción Ciudadana/Citizen's Action Party: nascent left-leaning political party in Costa Rica founded in 2000 whose candidate, Guillermo Solís, won the 2014 presidential elections on a platform that pushed anti-corruption as the main issue; colors are yellow and red

Partido de Unidad Socialcristiana/Social Christian Unity Party: center-right, minority political party founded in Costa Rica in 1977 that upholds a Christian democratic party line. The party was one of two dominant parties until the election of 2006, when elections were no longer divided along two-party lines; colors are blue and red

Partido Liberación Nacional (PLN)/National Liberation Party: long-standing, majority, center-left political party founded in Costa Rica in 1951 that promotes democratic socialism; colors are green and white, from which they derive their nickname "verdiblanco"—the green and whites

Patronato Nacional de la Infancia (PANI)/National Children's Trust: national Costa Rican institution that upholds the rights and conditions for minors

Patronio/patrón: drug lord or narcotics trafficking boss

Pelota(s): ball; in plural it is slang for male genitalia

Pereza: laziness, sloth, without desire to do something

Precario: Costa Rican term for a low-income squatter settlement mostly comprised of corrugated metal houses. It comes from the equivalent of "precarious" in Spanish, testament to the uncertainty surrounding life in poverty.

Puchero/puchera: local-level drug vendor

Puertas abiertas: open doors; refers to the expectation by gang members that their neighbors' doors are "always open" for any kind of favor or extortion payment. It is also a euphemism for loyalty of non-gang members to a particular gang in the controlled territory, usually as a result of fear.

Pulpería: corner store that sells packaged food items, snacks, and odds and ends

Pura Vida: commonly used Costa Rican phrase meaning "pure life," often used to say hello, thank you, have a good day, among other minor conversational terms. Used in the negative sense, it can refer to ignoring problems one's own surroundings in favor of discussing only the positive aspects.

Rancho: an undeveloped plot of land

Ranflero: low-level administrator who is part of the decision-making body within the *clika*, also known as "primera palabra," which is the first informal approval a *chequeo* must obtain while they seek initiation into the gang

Rito de iniciación: rite of initiation; refers to the process by which a *chequeo* is initiated into the gang as a full member. For young men, the rite includes a beating by several of his fellow gang members, usually in a circle, that lasts for the duration of a particular song, or it is measured using the count of a number of physical hits to the subject that is considered meaningful for the gang. For example, M-18 will often use thirteen, or multiples of it. MS-13 uses the number eighteen and seven. Fourteen is also a commonly used number because of its significance in Mayan culture from which many Central Americans derive their lineage—see also *Norteño* and *Mara Salvatrucha*). Young female *chequeos* can be initiated the same way. Young men beat young women as well. They often have a choice of becoming a sexual servant just for the leader(s) of the *clika* or for the whole group, though normative rules and morality governing gender roles within the gang are gang specific. This beating process is referred to as *ser brincado*, or to be "jumped into" the gang, whereas the rite can also include mythological, symbolic, religious elements, depending on the gang. To be jumped into the gang was a highly anticipated moment for many *chequeos* because it meant they would have less criminal work and fewer killings to perform once initiated and could benefit from the work of other *chequeos*. It was also a status symbol and a passage toward acceptance, thereby filling a need for belonging (*pertenecia*). As many as four people could be initiated on the same day within a gang. Some die in the process of initiation; others emerge with severe injuries.

Rompecabezas: puzzle; the literal translation is "head break" and can refer metaphorically to something that is confusing, paradoxical, or challenging.

Sala IV: Constitutional Chamber of the Supreme Court that decides the most urgent legal matters in the caseload

Salón: house or other site that serves as a meeting place for the clika where already-initiated gang members spend time during the day, smoke marijuana, eat, and plan attacks or extortion exercises. Some privileged gang members might also sleep there. The *salon* was also the location for the gang's parties and prostitution. This place is also known as a "destroyer."

Salvatrucha: literally means "saved trout," the national fish of El Salvador; Mara Salvatrucha (MS-13), which originated in El Salvador, uses the imagery of a species of fish whose eggs are hatched downstream and must swim vigorously upstream once birthed. The gang uses this imagery to represent how members are fighting for survival, encounter many challenges along the way, and that many do not survive the journey.

Segunda palabra: meaning "second word," refers to those members of the administration of a *clika* who observe the *chequeos* alongside members deemed to have *tercera palabra* to see if the younger members are ready to pass the rite of initiation

Soda: typical Costa Rican restaurant that serves *casados*, or the day's main meal, among items like candy, cigarettes, sodas, and snacks

Soldados: any group of members operating in the drug trade value chain that does not work directly for the narcotics trafficking boss, a direct translation is "foot soldiers"

Sombrero: wide-brimmed hat

Sicario: hitman

Tajada: cut of the financial earnings from a drug sale paid to the drug runners, vendors, and sometimes corrupt law enforcement officials

Techos prestados: literally means "borrowed roofs" and refers to the practice of gang members forcing neighbors to allow them to use their homes for shelter when they are being pursued by a rival gang or enemy

Tercera palabra: literally means "third word," refers to the most powerful members of a gang's *clika* who control the financial and material resources of the group, set rules and norms according to those observed by leaders higher in the gang, and guide activities of the gang. They make the final decision as to whether a *chequeo* can be initiated into the gang.

Territorio: territory; refers to the area of land that is controlled by a particular gang. Gang units can lose territory in "gang wars" with other neighboring gangs. *Clikas* can charge organized criminal groups for use of their land, particularly if the group wants to traffic materials or people through the area. In this sense, gangs also function as gatekeepers of public property in some cases.

Veterano: gang members that originated in Central America, traveled to the United States, and were deported back to their country of origin. These members are perceived as weaker and less aggressive than their counterparts who never left. *Veteranos* cannot usually assume a position of leadership among the gang unit they return to.

Vigilante: individual that watches out for the security of the *puchero* or local-level drug dealer

APPENDIX

———

AUTHOR'S NOTE

Lustgarten, Abrahm. "The Great Climate Migration Has Begun." *The New York Times Magazine*. July 23, 2020.
https://www.nytimes.com/interactive/2020/07/23/magazine/climate-migration.html.

Translated Facebook direct message to author. January 29, 2020.

AFTERWORD

BAHNVI—Mortgage Loan Bank of Costa Rica. "Historical Review." Accessed February 23, 2021.
https://www.banhvi.fi.cr/quienes_somos/resena_historica.aspx.

Barrantes, Alberto C. "Days Are Numbered for Precario to Make Way for Beltway." *La Nación*. January 14, 2014.
https://www.nacion.com/el-pais/servicios/precario-tiene-los-dias-contados-para-dar-paso-a-circunvalacion/QIWCK23DK5DBXDLTNIOFZHIA6A/story/.

Barrantes, Alberto C. "INVU President Denounces 'Monopoly' in Social Welfare Houses." *La Nación*. June 3, 2014.
http://www.nacion.com/nacional/Presidenta-INVU-denuncia-monopolio-social_0_1418458165.html.

Clemens, Michael. "The Real Economic Cost of Accepting Refugees." *Center for Global Development*. September 14, 2017.
https://www.cgdev.org/blog/real-economic-cost-accepting-refugees.

Costa Rica Ministry of Health. "The Eviction of Triángulo de Solidaridad Reached Its Conclusion Today." September 10, 2019.
https://www.ministeriodesalud.go.cr/index.php/noticias/noticias-2019/1475-desalojo-de-triangulo-de-solidaridad-llego-hoy-a-su-conclusion.

Costa Rica Ministry of Housing and Human Settlements (MIVAH). "Report on the Updating of Precario Settlements in the Greater Metropolitan Area." February 2005.

DAC List of ODA Flows. s.v. "Costa Rica." By Organization for Economic
Co-operation and Development (OECD). Accessed February 15, 2021.
http://www.oecd.org/dac/financing-sustainable-development/development-finance-
standards/DAC-List-ODA-Recipients-for-reporting-2021-flows.pdf.

Domonoske, Camila. "Fall of the Tower of David: Squatters Leave Venezuela's
Vertical Slum." *National Public Radio (NPR) The Two Way.* July 23, 2014.
https://www.npr.org/sections/thetwo-way/2014/07/23/334613896/fall-of-the-tower-
of-david-squatters-leave-venezuelas-vertical-slum.

Gibson, Owen, and Jonathan Watts. "World Cup: Rio Favelas Being 'Socially
Cleansed' in Runup to Sporting Events." *The Guardian.* December 5, 2013.
https://www.theguardian.com/world/2013/dec/05/world-cup-favelas-socially-
cleansed-olympics.

Horowitz, Juliana Menasce, Ruth Igielnik, and Rakesh Kochhar. *Most Americans
Say There Is Too Much Economic Inequality in the US, but Fewer Than Half Call It a
Top Priority,* (Washington, DC: Pew Research Center, 2020), 1.
https://www.pewsocialtrends.org/2020/01/09/trends-in-income-and-wealth-inequality/.

Keep, Ewart, and Ken Mayhew. "Inequality—'Wicked Problems,' Labor Market
Outcomes and the Search for Silver Bullets." *Oxford Review of Education* 40, no. 6
(2014): 764-781.

Ijjasz-Vasquez, Ede, Soraya Goga, and Ellen Hamilton. "Refugees and Internally
Displaced Persons in Cities—The 'Hidden' Side of Forced Displacement." *World
Bank (blog).* May 22, 2019. Accessed February 15, 2021.
https://blogs.worldbank.org/sustainablecities/refugees-and-internally-displaced-
persons-cities-hidden-side-forced-displacement.

"Inequality Index: Where Are the World's Most Unequal Countries?" *The Guardian*
(blog). April 26, 2017. Accessed February 15, 2021.
https://www.theguardian.com/inequality/datablog/2017/apr/26/inequality-index-
where-are-the-worlds-most-unequal-countries.

Lederach, John Paul. *The Moral Imagination: The Art and Soul of Building Peace.*
Oxford, UK: Oxford University Press, 2005, 55.

Liberoff, Jenny, Cinthia Carpio, and Lizeth Venegas. Costa Rica Ministry of
Housing and Human Settlements (MIVAH). "Proposal for an Intervention Model in
Triángulo de Solidaridad." May 2011.

Mata Blano, Alonso. "Poems and Troubles in the Decline of Precario Triángulo de
Solidaridad." *La Nacion.* June 1, 2014.
http://www.nacion.com/ocio/revista-dominical/Poesias-apuros-precario-
Triangulo-Solidaridad_0_1418058202.html.

"North Beltway Forces the Expropriation of Thirty Companies." *La Nación.* April 9, 2014.
http://www.nacion.com/nacional/transportes/Circunvalacion-norte-obliga-
expropiar-empresas_0_1407459282.html.

Panja, Tariq. "Brazil World Cup Stadium Could Be Used for Prisoners, Judge Says."
Bloomberg News. September 24, 2013.
https://www.bloomberg.com/news/articles/2013-09-24/brazil-world-cup-stadium-
could-be-used-for-prisoners-judge-says.

Rigaud, Kanta Kumari, Alex de Sherbinin, Bryan Jones, Jonas Bergmann, Viviane Clement, Kayly Ober, Jacob Schewe, Susana Adamo, Brent McCusker, Silke Heuser, and Amelia Midgley. *Groundswell: Preparing for Internal Climate Migration.* Washington, DC: The World Bank, 2018, 2.

Sandin, Linnea. "COVID-19 Exposes Latin America's Inequality." *Center for Strategic International Studies (CSIS).* April 6, 2020. https://www.csis.org/analysis/covid-19-exposes-latin-americas-inequality#:~:text=Of%20the%2020%20most%20economically,are%20classified%20as%20high%20income.

Sequeira, Aarón. "Defender Resigns Two Months after Her Re-Election." *La Nación.* July 8, 2014. http://www.nacion.com/nacional/politica/Defensora-renuncia-meses-nombramiento_0_1425457503.html.

Scott, Anna. "Homelessness in Los Angeles County Rises Sharply." National Public Radio (NPR). June 12, 2020. https://www.npr.org/2020/06/12/875888864/homelessness-in-los-angeles-county-rises-sharply.

Simon, Romero, and Christopher Clarey. "Note to Olympic Sailors: Don't Fall in Rio's Water." *The New York Times.* May 18, 2014. https://www.nytimes.com/2014/05/19/world/americas/memo-to-olympic-sailors-in-rio-dont-touch-the-water.html.

Strozenberg, Pedro. "Brazil: 'This Is a Moment of Fragility for Civil Society.'" *CIVICUS.* April 25, 2019. https://www.civicus.org/index.php/media-resources/news/interviews/3836-brazil-this-is-a-moment-of-fragility-for-civil-society.

Summers, Andy. "The New Bottom Billion: What If Most of the World's Poor Live in Middle-Income Countries?" *Center for Global Development.* March 18, 2011. Accessed February 28, 2021. https://www.cgdev.org/sites/default/files/1424922_file_Sumner_brief_MIC_poor_FINAL.pdf.

Ulibarri P., Eloísa, Carmen González A., Anayansy Valverde, Rodolfo Gutiérrez, Rosendo Pujol, and Jorge Solano. *Eleventh Report on the State of the Nation on Sustainable Human Development: Housing and Precario Settlements in the Greater Metropolitan Area (GAM), Final Report.* Costa Rica: Foundation for Housing Promotion (FUPROVI), 2005.

United Nations High Commissioner for Refugees (UNHCR). "Figures at a Glance." Accessed February 15, 2021. https://www.unhcr.org/en-us/figures-at-a-glance.html.

Made in the USA
Middletown, DE
16 May 2021